HELLIONS AT LARGE

Calvin Simpson was in trouble when, after chasing the thief Slim Tillot, he failed to keep his rendezvous with his brother Bob who was taking the payroll to the Circle S ranch . . . Bob and the money disappeared, and when Bob was found dead without the payroll, Cal was held responsible . . . A search involved Cal in clashes with two escaped convicts and their deadly half-brother, Forest Jack, before the Circle S was freed from the attentions of the malicious outlaw interlopers.

DAVID BINGLEY

HELLIONS AT LARGE

Complete and Unabridged

LINFORD
Leicester

First published in Great Britain in 1969

First Linford Edition
published 2006

British Library CIP Data

Bingley, David
    Hellions at large.—Large print ed.—
Linford western library
    1. Western stories
    2. Large type books
    I. Title
    823.9'14 [F]

    ISBN 1–84617–240–3

Published by
F. A. Thorpe (Publishing)
Anstey, Leicestershire

Set by Words & Graphics Ltd.
Anstey, Leicestershire
Printed and bound in Great Britain by
T. J. International Ltd., Padstow, Cornwall

This book is printed on acid-free paper

1

The sun was a brassy disc in the sky above the well-marked trail as the two young riders covered the last half mile of their ride into the town of Wildcat, in Gila County, south-west of New Mexico territory.

Although they had not ridden more than three miles at an easy pace, a fine dust covered them and their muscular mounts.

The Simpson brothers, joint heirs to the extensive Circle S ranch, north-east of town, had travelled most of the way in silence. Bob, the older of the two, was twenty-six years of age. He surveyed the trail through steady blue eyes under tufted brows. His habit of adjusting his undented dun stetson revealed a good head of bushy fair hair which would last him all his life. His broad shoulders were draped in a check shirt and loose black vest. He had a full, straight nose and a pointed jaw, which he massaged from time to time with a gauntleted hand.

The stockingfoot roan which carried Bob snorted occasionally and sidestepped towards the sorrel gelding which carried Calvin, the younger brother.

Cal's hair was auburn in colour and he wore it short with tapering sideburns. He had the same family features, namely the long full nose and pointed jaw, but his eyes were green, and his shoulders were sloping and muscular. He was thick in the chest rather than broad, and the corners of his mouth often puckered as though he was going to smile.

Cal glanced at Bob, who nodded to him.

'I'll be glad when we hit town an' get this chore over,' Bob murmured, licking his dry lips.

'You'll stay in town long enough to take a glass or two of beer, won't you, Bob?'

Bob sounded anxious. 'Sure, Cal, I'll get rid of the thirst an' then take myself along to the bank. Gettin' the payroll back to the spread is an important chore. I don't want to delay makin' the return, so I'm hopin' you won't feel drawn to watch any of that prize-fightin' on an occasion like this.'

Flexing the muscles of his arms and shoulders, Cal thought about the prize ring and the smell of sawdust, and all the trappings of the art of self-defence. Boxing was a pastime with him, and he had dearly hoped to watch a bout or two, or even to take part, if there was a call for volunteers.

He noted that Bob's jaw had tightened a little. It was no use to protest against big brother's decision to get back in a hurry. Of course, he was right. The payroll was over a thousand dollars, and it had to be returned safely to the ranch. Henry, their father, was getting to an age when he worried if they were a little overdue with the pay for the hands.

'So how long do you think you'll want to slake your thirst an' collect from the bank?'

'An hour, no more,' Bob replied soberly. 'The bank manager will have the cash ready. There shouldn't be any delay on that score.'

Side by side they jogged under the welcome sign which was nailed across the street between the two end buildings on either side of Main.

'I'll expect you at the bank, then,' Bob added.

'I'll try not to disappoint you, brother,' Cal replied drily.

The younger brother put his rowels lightly to the gelding's flanks and drew away. Soon the sorrel was turning off at an intersection. Cal's love for fisticuffs was drawing him to the marquee on the town square, even before he had slaked his thirst.

To right and left people on foot and mounted, or in carts, glanced in his direction and nodded. Cal touched his hat from time to time, but he was anxious to get to the big tent without any loss of time.

A man with his hands thrust in his pockets shouted a word of advice. 'The liveries are mostly full, mister, you might as well leave that bronc hitched to a rail — if you're headin' where I think you are!'

Cal acknowledged the advice and acted upon it. He swung the sorrel to a rail in front of a steamy eating house, and hitched it to a post which had been well chewed by horses awaiting their masters in the past. There was a stone trough of water within the animal's reach, and it received some comfort when the saddle was slackened.

Upwards of a score of adults milled around the entrance to the marquee. A barker with a cigar in the corner of his mouth was shouting about the attractions within. At that time, two lightweights were fighting for a small but useful purse. Soon, two of the star attractions, Sailor McCardoe and Battling Barnes, would be in the ring and there was not a lot of spare room for latecomers.

Cal hesitated without quite knowing why. As he did so, a stoop-shouldered man in the rig of the average cowpuncher came through the crowd of visitors, jostled him, stepped aside and moved on again, lowering his eyes and almost darting away. Cal blinked and peered after him, recognition coming slowly. He was seeing the face in other circumstances. It was a lined visage, that of a man of thirty-five with thinning dark hair and a drooping moustache.

Cal pointed after the fellow and called him by name. 'Hey, Slim! Slim Tillot, hold on there! You have unfinished business with the Circle S!'

The hurrying man must have heard his name called. He did not turn around, but ducked into an alleyway between two buildings. Cal went after him, but he had to push his way through still more men bent on getting to the marquee. Consequently, Tillot had disappeared across the open ground behind the buildings by the time Cal reached the other end of the alley.

The younger Simpson pulled up short, breathing hard and adjusting the undented dun stetson which was so like his brother's. Slim Tillot had led the Circle S outfit a dance. He had proved himself totally unreliable as a waddy, and he had finally left in disgrace, but not until he had filled his pockets with the belongings of other men.

Upwards of a hundred dollars of the hands' money had gone with him, and also one or two small pocketable items out of the ranch house itself. One item in particular had angered old Henry Simpson. That had been a gold ring with the Circle S emblem engraved on the inside.

When the thefts occurred some six months earlier, Cal had pursued the thief into town, but Tillot's start had been enough for him to clear town again and make himself scarce before

7

the vengeful Simpsons or the law could bring him to justice. Now, it seemed, he had returned, trusting to the crowded state of the town to mask him from the wary-eyed peace officers who were overworked at such times.

Cal thought about the fights going on in the marquee ring. Fights organized under the Marquess of Queensbury rules, which had originated in England in 1866. He would dearly have loved to watch, and also to participate, if there was any call for volunteers, but the honour of the Simpsons was at stake in the matter of Slim Tillot, and he steadfastly took up the chase.

After crossing the rear of one building, he returned to the cross section and hurried down the sidewalk. Slim had tricked him, but he would have to reappear on one of the streets again before very long. Back on Main, Cal turned left, and kept close to the fronts of the buildings so that he was partially hidden by the shade.

Fifty yards up the street, he had a

spot of luck. Tillot emerged again, glanced furtively in both directions, and carried on in the direction which Cal had been taking. The auburn-haired young man kept quite still for a few seconds. He moved forward only when others were masking his movements by coming the other way.

Presently, Tillot crossed the dirt and went up onto the boards at the other side. After glancing around once again, he opened the door of a shop and slipped inside. Cal slowed again. He knew the shop, and he was quite content to wait until Slim came out.

He felt in his pocket, pulled out his tobacco sack and busied his fingers with the rolling of a smoke. He put the cigarette between his lips but did not light it. He was recollecting that smoking was not good for a fighting man's wind.

For a time, he waited with his shoulder resting against a post. Then, after five minutes, he became restless again. Slim had not emerged, and the minutes of the valuable hour in town were slipping away. He crossed to the other side, ambled along to the shop where the thief had disappeared and glanced at the items in the window.

Dan Marks, the shopkeeper, was a mild-mannered fellow of sixty, rather deaf and certainly short-sighted without his gold-rimmed spectacles. He wore a dark business suit and an embroidered skull cap over a good head of white hair. As Cal watched, Marks put his head through the curtains at the back of the window.

The shopkeeper glanced at him over his spectacles and leaned forward to place a new object in the foreground of the display. Amid the jewellery, clocks — new and second-hand — and other items of the nature of luxury and fancy goods, the ring in the black velvet display stand did not stand out very much. But Cal had been thinking about his father's stolen ring, and so he bent down to take a close look at the object as Mark's head was withdrawn.

Men's thick, solid gold rings tend to look very much alike to the eyes of ordinary observers. But Cal looked twice. He frowned because a good half of the inside of the ring was hidden by the velvet in which it was held. Fleeting thoughts left him troubled. He was wondering if Slim Tillot would have the nerve to bring the Circle S ring back into Wildcat, a town so close to where it had been stolen.

Moreover, would he be rash enough to actually pawn the ring with Wildcat's leading second-hand dealer?

Cal's anger increased. He glanced through the door of the shop. It was comparatively dark in there, compared with the brightness of the open air. Nevertheless, he thought he ought to have been able to see Slim Tillot somewhere around. The shop appeared to be empty. Even the owner had gone through to the rear.

Acting on impulse, Cal opened the door and stepped inside. He had been right. There was no sign of the elusive fellow he had seen go into the shop. He waited by the counter until old Dan Marks came out again, gently nodding his head as he walked.

'Young Mr Simpson, ain't it? Anythin' I can do for you today, Cal?'

Marks spread his hands and leaned across from the back of the counter. Cal's eyes went from the proprietor to the window and then to the rear door by which the old man had entered.

'Howdy, Mr Marks. You had a customer jest a few minutes ago. I was hankerin' after a short chat with him. What became of him? I didn't see him come out.'

Marks chuckled and shook his head. 'He concluded his business an' politely asked permission to leave by my rear entrance. So you see, there's no mystery.'

Cal, standing there biting his underlip, looked anything but satisfied. He said: 'Did he by any chance sell you the ring you jest put in the window?'

Marks nodded, and Cal asked to see

it. The old man was rubbing his hands as his visitor examined it. It was not often that he turned over a piece of merchandise in so short a time. Cal carried it towards the window and held it up to the light, above the curtain. Clearly, inside the ring he could see a symbol, but it was not the symbol he had expected. He gave a sharp exclamation and returned with it to the counter.

'Dan, this has a figure eight inside a circle. I could have sworn it was a ring stolen from my Pa. But if that were so, there should have been an S in the circle, not a figure eight. Do you have one of those jewellers' glasses for taking a close look at precious things?'

Marks' face had hardened. He produced a glass from his coat pocket, screwed it into his eye, and felt for the lamp hanging above his head. Rasping a match on the seat of his trousers, the old man lit the lamp and commenced his examination.

After an examination lasting some thirty seconds, Marks nodded. 'You're right, Cal. The eight has been altered from something else, and so far as I can see it must have been an S. So this could have been your Pa's ring? Was it my customer who stole it?'

'Certainly it was. About six months ago. Only he skipped town ahead of me, an' I didn't figure to see the ring, or him, any more. Now, he's turned up again, an' he must have a nerve to sell the ring, right under my nose. I'll have to go after him. You didn't see which way he went, did you?'

'No, I didn't,' Marks returned gravely, 'but his hands had a smell of resin. I'd say he had something to do with the prize-fighters over in the marquee. I believe they use resin these days to rub on their boots, so that they won't slip on the canvas.'

Cal's spirits were boosted. He grinned, asked Marks to keep the ring for him, and hurried out of the door, feeling sure that he could find the fellow again and hand him over to the Town Marshal to stand trial.

At the entrance to the marquee, he had trouble. The tent was packed and no one else was allowed in. Only when a dollar had changed hands did one of the men on the gate admit to having seen a man answering Tillot's description with one of the heavyweight boxers' outfits.

A brief consultation elicited the name of Battling Barnes, a strong, stocky man with a scarred face. Barnes had a reputation for being very hard to beat. He could absorb a lot of punishment, and the fact that he was slightly below average height did not seem to prevent him from winning fights. He came from the Pacific coast and his reputation had preceded him.

Cal made it to Barnes' dressing room by walking round the marquee and simply asking for the boxer. A man acting as second cautiously admitted him, and Cal found himself in a small area which held the boxer, his manager, two seconds and the missing thief, Slim Tillot.

The man with the grizzled chin, who had admitted him, demanded to know more details.

Cal pointed. 'My business is not with Barnes, it's with that hombre over there, Slim Tillot. He's a thief, an' he's jest sold a ring he stole from my Pa.'

Tillot's face blanched. He moved warily along the canvas as far away from Cal as he could manage. The other men there looked to Barnes for a lead. As the others stood back and Cal lunged forward, Barnes stood up and barred his way. Tillot dropped to the ground, and began to crawl under the canvas wall.

'I'll have to ask you to step aside, Mr Barnes. The thief is gettin' away.'

Barnes, by way of reply, stuck out his chest and glared into Cal's face. 'He's a friend of mine. Besides, he ain't called Tillot, or whatever you said. You're mistaken.'

Barnes flexed his arms; his fists,

hidden in the leather gloves which had only recently been introduced into prize-fighting in the territory, looked huge. Most men would have backed off, in the circumstances, but Cal, a fighter himself, merely stepped back half a pace and showed his impatience.

'You're the one who's mistaken. An' you're allowin' a criminal to escape. Out of my way, Barnes.'

There was a silent backing off of the other men. Barnes ducked into a crouch and came forward. He waited until he was sure that Cal was within his reach, then he threw two heavy punches; first a left and then a right, at the head. Cal ducked under both, and as he came up he landed a stinging right hand just above the other's belt.

Although he was fit, Barnes winced. In the instant his eyes were shut, Cal connected with his jaw, throwing a long left lead. Then he closed and hit with his right over the heart. Rather belatedly, Barnes thought about a clinch, but by then an uppercut had rocked him. The punch which followed caught him squarely on the angle of the jaw, and sent him crashing sideways.

His head hit the wooden seat on which he had been sitting and the combined blows and the bump were sufficient to rob him of his senses.

2

For almost a minute there was silence in the tiny enclosure. It was as though everyone in the space had been struck dumb. Then, quite abruptly, everything changed. A roar went up in the ring area as the contest finished and the verdict was given.

While the spectators were shouting at one another over the result, Chad Martin, the fight promoter, slipped into Barnes' dressing room and pulled up short. Behind him, another official crowded in and stopped short with his mouth agape.

'What — what happened to Barnes?'

'Yer,' echoed Martin, a rugged ex-army man of fifty-six, 'what happened to the renowned heavyweight, eh? Jest when we want him in the ring.'

The manager fidgetted with his string tie. He nodded towards Cal, who immediately owned up to the fact that he had knocked Barnes senseless.

'He asked for trouble. I was on the point of apprehending a thief, an' Barnes interfered! Now, the jasper has slipped away again. He could clear town like he did last time! It ain't often we get a second chance with a clever thief!'

'Cal Simpson, you're a menace!' Martin told him. 'Are you tryin' to ruin me, an' spoil this fight bill? Do you realize what you've done? Barnes is due in the ring right now, in the top contest of the day. What'll I tell the crowd when he don't show up?'

Cal showed a certain amount of embarrassment. He shifted his feet uneasily. 'Best thing you can do, Mr Martin, is tell them the truth. Say he acted a little unwisely, and hit his head on a bench. Anyway, if the crowd can wait maybe he'll come round an' be fit to fight.'

At this latter suggestion the manager showed a flicker of renewed interest, but it was not shared by the promoter or his friend. The last man to arrive was talking in a whisper into the promoter's ear. His moustache was mingling with a tuft of hair and irritating Martin's ear, but the words appeared to be pleasing.

The promoter slapped his thigh. 'That's what we'll do. It's the only way. Barnes, there, is still glass-eyed. Simpson, here, will have to take his place. After all, he's partly to blame for what has occurred. You hear me, Cal? You're goin' in the ring with Sailor McCardoe, so get yourself ready. An' don't tell me you ain't interested in prize-fightin' 'cause I know different.'

'But Mr Martin, I'm trying to catch a thief!' Cal protested.

The manager's protest was an elaborate mime. Meanwhile, poor Barnes began to recover his senses, largely due to the ministrations of his fussing seconds. They planted him on the seat and wiped his face and neck with a wet sponge.

At that moment, Martin pushed his

friend back into the marquee proper, and made as if to follow him. He addressed Barnes' manager.

'You, mister, see Simpson here is ready in five minutes. Get a pair of gloves on his hands an' bring him along. If the crowd gets out of hand, they'll be here to collect you an' they won't be gentle either.'

Seconds later, the hubbub of impatient men changed to a shout of protest as the change in the bill was announced.

Martin took over the announcing from the centre of the ring.

'Folks, you shouldn't be disappointed with Cal Simpson. I know he ain't a full professional, but he boxes well, an' he'd make a good substitute for any heavyweight in this area. When he comes into the ring, I want you to give him a great big hand.'

And the crowd responded as he had asked, having got over their disappointment about being cheated out of the McCardoe-Barnes maul.

Cal was full of excitement. He had been forced into this fight, and he was going to do his best. Circumstances had contrived this match, and that was good enough for him. Slim Tillot and brother Bob were relegated to the back of his mind for a time. He was going to give the crowd a decent show, if he could.

A flicker of conscience over Tillot was salved by the knowledge that Pa's ring had been recovered. The arrival of Sailor McCardoe brought everything to fever heat. Sailor was a tall lean man in his late twenties with weather-tanned features and an exceptionally long pair of workmanlike arms. He was as keen to see his substitute opponent as Cal was to see him.

After taking a bow, they eyed each other from diagonally opposite corners and wondered how the fight would go. The announcer reminded spectators that the original fight was scheduled for ten rounds, and that Simpson had not questioned the duration since he elected to substitute. The fight could still be a long one.

McCardoe was slowly shaking his head. His seconds were grinning, especially as the original purse was there for the winning, in spite of Barnes' unfortunate demise. The shouting of the crowd began again as the announcer retired and the referee, a man with a clean hairless skull, took over.

Soon, the preliminaries were concluded, and the fighters were left standing in their corners, shadow boxing and anxious to begin. The bell clanged and they came forward, touched gloves and began their sparring.

Two minutes were spent in careful weaving and dodging. At the end of that time, McCardoe appeared to be satisfied with his survey of the unknown opponent. He had formed the conclusion that Cal was fit, but that he had no punches worthy of note, and no special tricks.

Twice in the last few seconds, that

extra long reach enabled McCardoe to land on Cal's face. Small bruises began to form on his jaw and cheekbone. Barnes' seconds, who were acting for him, were only half-hearted in their attentions in the first interval.

Some thirty seconds had gone by in round two when McCardoe aimed a punch straight at Cal's mouth. He slid away from it, but received a puffed lip. For almost another minute, the local boy backed away, and the crowd began to shout for him to go forward.

Around the two minutes' mark, Cal slipped a left lead that came out like a whiplash. He stepped in close, landed a one-two in the lanky man's chest and clipped him with an uppercut as the long arms sought to embrace him. Seconds slipped by as McCardoe waited with his eyes slightly glazed.

Cal feinted with his right, threw a left which went through to the chin, and ripped in two vicious rights to the other's solar plexus. McCardoe's experience had never subjected him to an attack so low down. He slid to the canvas, writhing and struggling for breath and did not get his feet under him until the referee had counted ten and held up Cal's hand. Ears throbbed with the uproar which came from the watchers. They had forgotten their disappointment about Barnes, forgotten for a time, also, that the contest had been short-lived.

Cal made a round of the ring, waving his hand, and then slipped under the ropes in his borrowed shorts and boots and headed back for his outdoor clothes. He found that Barnes had gone out for a drink when he reached the dressing room. Barnes' manager, still looking rather disgusted, kept out of his way as he dressed and showed no special interest until Promoter Martin came into the area with Cal's winnings. He handed over fifty dollars, and stood back, shaking his head.

'If only you Simpsons weren't always in such an all-fired hurry,' he grumbled. 'You could have sparred around, kept out of trouble for several rounds, and then put Sailor on the canvas later in the fight! Anyway, if you ever want a paid fight or two after this, get in touch, young fellow. Things haven't turned out too badly after all. I hope you catch your thief.'

Martin shook hands and left. Before putting away his winnings, Cal peeled off twenty dollars and handed them to the manager, telling him to use them for expenses. Pocketing the rest, he went out into the open and took a quick turn around the main buildings.

As he had expected, Tillot had completely disappeared. He was nowhere to be seen, and no one claimed to have seen him, either. A prey to mixed feelings, Cal went back to Marks' store and paid ten dollars for his father's ring. He asked Marks to make known to the town marshal how Tillot had brought in the stolen ring, and also asked that a lookout might be kept for the thief. Marks closed up his shop to do the message, and Cal returned to the spot where he had left his gelding.

He received a cool reception from the animal, and an even cooler one from the bank manager, who informed him that Bob had waited for him, and then left for home in rather a bad temper some thirty minutes earlier.

Cal's brow clouded. He licked his lips, thought about the beer that he would have liked to have drunk, and rather dejectedly set off for home.

The first half mile was easy-going. After that, the terrain coarsened as the private track headed through semi-wild and rugged territory towards the Circle S lands. Cal pushed the sorrel, but he made no impression upon the rider up ahead. A fine sheen of dust showed that Bob had, in fact, preceded him, but at none of the crests of the slight upgrades were any signs of the other rider visible.

Soon, two miles had gone by. At that stage, Cal began to grow anxious. The payroll was back in his thoughts again.

One man with a thousand dollars could easily be separated from it by determined men who took advantage of the rocky scrub-ridden ground, and who used the element of surprise.

Cal rode along shaking his head. That sort of thing did not happen to the Simpsons. The county had not suffered from raiders in the recent past. The settlers had no griping fears about coach robbers, rustlers or bank robbers. This had been the case for upwards of two years.

Cal pushed the sorrel hard. Its hide began to show signs of its exertion. On the last run in to the Circle S home buildings, doubts assailed him all over again. He pulled out his glass and focused it on the rail in front of the ranch house. Bob's stockingfoot ought to be there, if he had arrived. Not only was there no stockingfoot, there were no horses at all.

Sitting on the front gallery were his mother, Rebecca, his sister, Mollie, not long back from a finishing school in the east, and old Henry, his father. Even as he used the glass, Henry bobbed up out of his chair and shaded his eyes to see who was approaching.

Cal knew a chill feeling round his heart. If anything had happened to Bob, the folks on that gallery would never recover from the blow.

At fifty-six, Rebecca was a frail shell of a woman. Her grey hair was parted in the middle and pulled back in a severe style to the nape of her neck. Privations in the early days, when she and Henry had first moved west, had robbed her of her robust health. Her cheeks were thin, her weight was low. Her high colouring gave a hint at weak circulation and heart trouble.

Henry was three years younger. He was still strong, though inactive in recent years since he injured a hip during a horse-breaking exercise. His grey hair was turning white. His troubled face resembled cracked parchment.

Mollie, the youngest of the three Simpson offspring, was a bright-eyed copper-headed girl with a long straight bell of hair down to her shoulders. At the time of Cal's approach, she was wearing a white shirt and tight black denim trousers.

Henry's eyesight was good at distances, in spite of the time he spent reading books. He picked out Cal's features without difficulty and the knowledge that his younger son was approaching alone did nothing to ease his troubled mind. He pulled out his gold hunter from the pocket of his grey vest and flicked open the cover. Cal was late, late enough to have left town *after* Bob.

Some fifty yards away, Cal waved his hat to the family, but he was not yet ready to go forward and express his fears. Instead, he opened the gate of the paddock, rode around to the nearest stable, and glanced in.

There was no sign of the stocking-foot. He was deluding himself. Bob had not arrived. The small Chinese cook came out of the next building and confirmed this.

He called: 'Mr Cal, there's coffee here waitin' if you want some. Is Mr Bob with you?'

'All right, Chang, maybe I'll drop in in a few minutes. No, Bob's not with me. I take it he ain't arrived yet?'

The cook shook his head and scuttled back into his work quarters, while Cal walked his horse towards the main building. Henry was leaning on the rail, glowering at him.

'Howdy, Pa, Ma and Mollie, it's a dry day, sure enough.'

'Well, Cal?' Henry snapped. 'Where's Bob an' that payroll?'

'I don't know, Pa, he must have left before me. You see, I caught sight of Slim Tillot in town, an' that delayed me. Here, do you recognize this?'

Grinning broadly, he pulled Henry's ring off his finger and handed it over. Henry was shaking his head and trying to get around to asking more questions.

'Somebody's altered the Circle S to Circle 8, but it's yours, all right. Ain't you pleased to get it back? It cost me all of ten dollars, Pa.'

'Eh? Yes, all right, son, but you're stallin'. You ain't tellin' me what I want to know. Now, about Bob an' the payroll.'

'He left before me, Pa. I was late on account of Tillot. But I didn't see Bob on the trail, an' I'm surprised he ain't here already. How would it be to send out a few of the boys to look around for him?'

'Keep your voice down,' Henry whispered curtly. 'Do you want to shock your mother?'

Mollie had risen from her chair and was taking Rebecca indoors. Patiently, she explained that Bob had been delayed. As soon as the women were out of earshot, the rancher vented his anger upon his son.

'Cal, doggone it, you've let us down! I don't believe Slim Tillot put that bruise on your cheek, or busted your lip. You've been along to the prize-fighting tent, an' now Bob's missin' and the money, too. You bring me a paltry gold ring an' expect me to be pleased when my son and heir is missin' and the monthly payroll?'

'I'll do what I can to make amends,' Cal offered.

'Go an' find Raybold, an' tell him to round up as many of the boys as he can. Tell him to start lookin'.'

Cal touched his hat and went off to do his father's bidding. Raybold was the ranch segundo. As such, he had a lot of time for Bob Simpson, but very little patience with Cal.

3

Two score riders turned out in answer to the master's summons. Henry headed one group, and Larry Raybold a second. Cal, more troubled perhaps than any of the others, elected to ride alone. He turned south of the town track and spent almost two hours looking into tiny draws and gullies which they had used as small boys. He found no sign at all to suggest that Bob had turned off in that direction.

At last, the call of duty made him turn around in order to return home and find out the worst. He felt certain in his own mind that the others would not have found sign either, but in that he was wrong.

As he walked his tired cayuse into the yard, the cook again put him in possession of the facts. Mr Bob, it appeared, had been spirited away, but his horse, the stockingfoot roan, had been found wandering in a small park of grass over a furlong north of the trail about half way between town and home.

Cal thanked him and dismounted. He walked his gelding towards the stable, and took it inside. Two people were looking over the roan, Raybold and Mollie. The girl was helping to groom it and Raybold was glad of her company.

He was saying: 'Miss Mollie, it don't do to jump to conclusions. If you think the worst you might communicate it to your mother. An' that wouldn't do.'

'By goodness, you're right, though, Larry,' Mollie replied. 'All of us are surely goin' to have to watch what we say, until he turns up. An' the worry is botherin' Pa, too.'

Cal's sudden appearance put a rein on the conversation. One shrewd glance at Cal's face told them the worst. Mollie surrendered the brush and came over to him. He put an arm round her and tried to comfort her, but this was hard to do under the withering glance which Raybold was giving him.

Raybold had never seemingly liked Cal, and now it was showing more. Moreover, the segundo seemed to have taken a marked fancy to Mollie since she returned from an eastern finishing school a few short months ago.

'Go on into the house, sis,' Cal suggested. 'I'll follow you in a minute.'

She smiled briefly and withdrew.

Cal moved closer to the roan. He said: 'The signs look bad, Larry.'

Raybold nodded. 'Before you came in I was sayin' to your sister that Mr Bob might have fallen an' hit his head or somethin' but you an' me, we don't need to wrap things up. Somebody's attacked him, an' stolen the money, an' for those who value his life more than the cash, it looks bad!'

'That's puttin' it very bluntly, but I fear you may be right,' Cal murmured unhappily. 'Do I take it you think I'm to blame for not bein' with him?'

'How else can I view the situation? I offered to go with him, but you insisted on goin' an' you said you didn't need me along. Your face says you've been in a fight. I'd say you put your prize-fightin' hobby above your brother's safety, an' that ranks a man pretty low from my point of view. Now, your folks have got to suffer, an' two of them ain't hearty enough to shrug off tragedy.'

'Maybe things ain't quite so black as all that,' Cal dared to suggest.

Before Raybold could say any more, Cal had tossed his saddle in a corner and left the building.

* * *

The following morning, Henry Simpson ordered Cal to ride back into town and collect more money for the hands' pay. He was also to inform the town marshal's office as to what had happened, and he was to keep Raybold right alongside of him all the time he was away.

Cal saw it as a kind of punishment, knowing that Raybold openly disliked him, but he carried out his task and it was not long after eleven o'clock when they started to approach the ranch again. Raybold was whistling disdainfully through his teeth.

Cal cleared his throat. 'Larry, I've endured the silent crticism of the bank manager, the town marshal an' others. Yours I can't altogether stomach. You sneer too easily.'

A couple of yards away, Raybold swayed with the easy step of his cayuse. 'You don't say, Mr Cal. An' what do you expect? Every man in town thinkin' you're a great hero with your fists when all the time you were lettin' your brother down. If your conscience is botherin' you, don't blame me because I'm not goin' to give you an excuse to use your fists on me.'

'You're wise on that score,' Cal pointed out with some heat. 'But understand this, when a man has a brother as fast with a gun as Bob, it

39

ain't nice to always be second best. That's why I took up fist fightin'. You, I take it, think you're the fastest gun on the ranch now that Bob's gone.'

'You might jest be right,' Raybold replied, with a nod. 'In fact, I might have been the fastest before Mr Bob left.'

To demonstrate his faith in himself, Raybold did a fast draw with his revolver. Cal had to admit the movement had a very professional look about it. His temper was smouldering, however, and as soon as he had reported to his father and left the payroll in the house, he sought out Raybold behind the stable again, and put to him an unexpected challenge.

'See if you can draw faster than I can, Larry! Right there, where you are standin', huh?'

As they were no more than six feet apart, the segundo looked surprised. 'You really think you can outdraw me? Really?'

'Let's try it,' Cal suggested.

Both men stood with their feet slightly apart, in a crouch which made it easy to lunge for the hip and the holster. They watched each other's eyes. Suddenly, Raybold telegraphed a move. Cal leapt forward without attempting to draw his weapon. As Raybold's Colt cleared leather and started to come up, Cal shot out his left leg and kicked the weapon flying into the air. Before Raybold could recover from his surprise, a bunched fist had connected with his jaw and sent him to the ground.

He knew he had been outwitted for the moment by this fast moving son of the Boss, and he was content not to further lose face by standing up and slugging it out with a better man.

'All right, Cal, so you put one over on me, but there'll be other times. I've got a long memory.'

Cal nodded. 'You've got a long tongue, too.' He turned on his heel and moved away towards the house.

* * *

Half an hour after the midday meal, which had been prepared as usual by the Mexican maid, Carmencita, Cal delivered his ultimatum to his father.

'Pa, I'm leavin' the spread for a while. Riders from town are searchin' for Bob, but I might have better luck. I shan't be back in a hurry, but don't worry over me. If there's any way of tracin' Bob, I'll do it.'

Mother and daughter exchanged glances, but remained silent at the table. Henry Simpson received his son's news with indifference. He was suffering enough over Bob's disappearance without being bothered about Cal's latest scheme. Perhaps if Cal went away for a while it might be possible to think more kindly about him when he returned.

'Go and look, if that's what you've decided to do, an' do a little growin' up while you're away. Get past the outlook which says every little dispute can be settled with a big bunched fist.'

'A big bunched fist is better than a flamin' gun!' Cal retorted hotly, but he regretted his words as soon as they had been uttered. His mother was wondering already if Bob had been shot. He packed a few things into his saddle pockets and said his farewells, leaving a half hour later.

As he rode towards the west, and then turned north in the area where the roan had been found, he reminded himself that he was looking for a thousand stolen dollars; also for his brother, probably by now lying dead somewhere. Money and a corpse. It was a thing he had to do, but no one could say it was a pleasant task.

All the time he was riding he was hating the circumstances which had plunged the Simpson family into this position. Hating the fact that no one really wanted to know how he had been manoeuvred into fighting Sailor McCardoe when he had wanted only to catch Tillot and make his way home.

Faces kept going through his mind. Who would want to hurt Bob? Who would rob him, or kill him? Cal thought he was searching for a face to hate as he thought over the situation. The only face which kept floating into his consciousness was that of Raybold, the segundo. A mobile face with alert dark eyes and a semi-circular scar wide of the left one. Raybold, when he grinned, showed uneven teeth in a lantern jaw which swept up to long blue-black sideburns. He was above average in height and thick-set, though his figure — in his early thirties — carried little superfluous flesh.

Cal pushed the irritating fellow out of his thoughts with some difficulty. He did not believe that Raybold had any real affection for Bob. In the past few weeks, the foreman had shown more interest in the Simpsons than he had since he started working for them. His growing interest had coincided with Mollie's return home from school. Perhaps he had aspirations in that direction, and perhaps that was why Cal came as near to hating Raybold as he had done to any man in his youthful career.

Two days later, all the forces of law and order had given up the purposeful search for the missing rancher's son. The county seat at Hillsburg in the south had been alerted, and a note was made of Bob's description and the make-up of the missing payroll. But hope had died officially. Bob had to be presumed dead and the money dispersed.

Cal, who was not anxious to face his fellows for a while, continued his personal search. He knew the rugged territory to the north-west of the home ranch, having lived in the area all his life. Great stretches of Gila County were still wild, being the type of land which repelled settlers. Bob had disappeared in one of them.

The land in which Cal searched was not even the type to attract trappers, or prospectors. Very few of that type of settler, who wanted to be well away from their fellows, graced the upper stretches of Gila County land.

Cal knew of one loner, and he intended to find him at all costs. After climbing down nearly a dozen rock fissures, and squinting into the depths of as many more, without result, the rider had come to the conclusion that his search was going to be fruitless, unless he met up with someone.

At two o'clock in the afternoon, on the third day, the gelding crested a low rugged ridge, pitted with pointed rocks like the back of some pre-historic animal. Cal checked it just over the crest and looked down upon the turgid creek which made the draw distinguishable and different from the many other draws in the deserted terrain.

He knew that he had found the home haunts of one Silas Gallon, a hunting, shooting and fishing old timer, who had done many jobs. A ride along the bank of the creek produced no result. Cal turned the gelding around and rode up a sloping path towards the timber on the eastern slope.

Gallon's shack was on the far side of the trees. The door was open and there were no signs of life, but he was in there. Cal hitched his mount and strode as far as the doorway, leaning his shoulder against the frame. Gallon was seated at his ricketty table with a small flat liquor bottle in front of him and a chipped cup close to his hand.

For several seconds, the old man did not even bother to look at the visitor, but tiny puffs of smoke came from the bowl of the cracked pipe which was clamped between his worn-down teeth.

Gallon was heavy featured and bald. He was clothed in tattered buckskin and a big flat hat which was pushed to the back of his head. His face was lined and a substantial jowl with several days growth of beard on it hung below his chin. Dropped pinches of brown snuff had soiled his shirt.

He turned a bloodshot eye towards

the door. 'You comin' in, mister?'

Cal nodded, grinned and stepped inside, planting his body on the only other upright chair. The room and the loft were dirty and foul to look upon.

'I'm Cal Simpson, fron the Circle S spread, some miles south-east, Silas. We haven't visited you lately.'

Gallon's brows rose. 'Ain't nobody visited me lately, son. Why did you come?'

Cal rolled a smoke. He did not give his reason until the tobacco was burning, but Gallon did not notice the delay.

'My brother's gone amissin', Silas, somewhere south of here. You bein' the only hombre domiciled in the district, I had to come to you.'

'Did you think he was here?'

'No, but you might know something. If there was foul play, the ambushers might have ridden this way. Now, have you seen anyone lately?'

'Nobody at all, mister. Nobody. But you're welcome to stay a while if you want a rest. Make yourself at home, why don't you?'

Cal nodded, grinned and began to stroll about. 'One or more men with a thousand dollars of Circle S money. Maybe lookin' for a place to hide a body, eh? How about round here? This area is empty enough. Where would they put it? In the trees, down by the creek?'

Cal was only talking, but he perceived a reaction in the rheumy eyes of the old man whom he had at first thought to be too far gone in drink to be of assistance.

'If you know anythin', Silas, maybe a few dollars would loosen your tongue, eh?'

'I'm not short of cash, damn you! I mean my needs are simple. Anything I've got to say, I'll say without the exchange of money.'

Cal stood in front of him. 'Well, then? Did you see anything suspicious, or maybe hear noises in the night? A man has to find his brother, even if he's

49

dead! You do understand that, don't you, Silas?'

Cal bent down and grabbed him by the lapel. His hand tightened on the material, but the look in Gallon's eyes stopped him from being more aggressive. Cal relaxed his grip again, certain that he was going to learn something.

Gallon dropped his gaze to the table and pushed his hat forward.

'I ain't sayin' it was a body. You understand that. But there was something. Something weighted, maybe a sack. Strangers went along there, not far from the big weepin' willow, upstream. They dumped it into the creek, watched it bubble and sink and then rode away again. I — I didn't have any truck with them myself. It's best that way in these lonely parts. Now, will you leave me alone for a while?'

Cal nodded and thanked him. He went and sat out of doors, with his back to the wall of the shack. He had a feeling that he had been given his first lead. A weighted object in the bottom of the creek. Easier and quicker than digging a hole, if the man or men were in a hurry and not too fussy.

The lone searcher liked swimming, but this was one swim he did not particularly fancy. He stretched out on the ground and gazed up at the sky, but his troubles were griping him and he could not settle for long.

4

Silas Gallon's creek was indeed a turgid
one. Cal moved along its banks on the
back of the sorrel and gazed at it for a
time, trying to see into the depths of the
deeper water near the middle. Where
the big weeping willow spread its
branches the waterway was between
forty and fifty feet across. On either side
the banks separated, giving a width of
something nearer seventy feet.

Horse and rider negotiated the
shallows on the near side. There was no
sign of a sack or other object to be seen.
The sorrel made the swim to the other
side, and Cal made his search of the
shallows near the other bank. An hour
slipped away without any progress being
made, except that the sorrel had slaked
its thirst and derived some benefit through
having water pass over its body.

Cal dismounted and walked about on

the west side. There was nothing else for it. He had put off a personal swim for as long as was possible. He would have to strip off and go in. The gelding watched him as he pulled off his vest and shirt and tossed aside his undented stetson.

Something in the animal's look made him check the saddle. The cinch had tightened up with the water's action. He slackened it, and patted the gelding on the rump, sending it off in search of bunch grass, which was not hard to find.

Stripped to his denims and heated by the steady rays of the sun, Cal waded into the water and hurriedly glanced up each side of the creek. No one was there to witness his lone search. He felt lonelier then than he had done at any time since he left the home spread. It was hard to know the reason for such a feeling. Bob had also swum well; perhaps that was why he felt this way.

In three feet of water, small stones began to slip from under his feet. He put up his hands and dived in, feeling the pleasant touch of the liquid and the eddying bubbles he had created. The sun made the bottom clear up to three feet, but deeper than that the visibility was murky.

Blowing water from his nostrils, Cal threw back his head and filled his lungs. He made the first of several dives, which took him down about six feet at first and then considerably deeper. After fifteen fruitless minutes spent in diving, he began to tire. The strain on his lungs was telling. He surfaced, stretched out on his back and spread his limbs. Like a starfish, he floated and rested, shutting his eyes to exclude the bright sky.

His ears were under water, and the dull boom was muted to him as a small, unexpected projectile ripped into the creek's surface within an inch of his exposed chest. He jerked upright, put down his legs and almost panicked. A bullet! Almost without thinking, he filled his lungs, ducked his head and dived down. As he did so, more bullets fired from somewhere up the east bank came darting at him. Every one went close but none touched him.

He had swallowed the air well down into his lungs, and his thoughts were busy with the problem of where to surface. Obviously, he wanted to be on the same bank as his horse, and his clothing. He varied his stroke, turning to the right and aiming for the west bank. The shelving wall under the water came at him. He made adjustments, scraping his chest on the rough stony bottom. Soon, he was in the shallower water and heading for the cover afforded by shrubs which overhung the creek bank. Using a lot of control, he surfaced, showing only his face and the top of his head. As he gulped in air, he wondered if he was visible to the hidden marksman on the other bank, and whether a well-aimed bullet was going to leave his father without a son.

It took a great effort to keep his face averted from the direction of danger, but he managed it. The firing appeared to have ceased. He spent a whole minute manoeuvring himself further among the reeds, and when several of them had mildly scratched his face he turned over with scarcely a ripple and stared at the hostile bank.

The nearest trees were quite a few yards up the slope. There was no sign of any movement among them. He reminded himself of his lucky escape, and how the markman had moved himself into position without the slightest indication of his presence.

He wondered about Silas. The old man was scarcely alert enough to have fired that near-lethal flurry of shots. Therefore, someone else must have been in the vicinity of his lonely home. Someone who had seen Cal arrive, or spotted him soon after. Someone who immediately classed himself as Cal's enemy.

His thoughts made interesting conjecture. Not many men would try to kill a man for swimming in a lonely creek.

The marksman had to have a good reason. Maybe he had told Silas to direct a searcher down to the creek to swim. Did that mean that Bob's body had never been there? If there had been something dumped in the creek, it had proved elusive. There was just an outside chance that a sack of some sort had been dumped there, but Cal was beginning to doubt it very seriously.

He wondered what he ought to do now. He was a long way from his weapons, and although he was probably now out of sight of the would-be killer, he would probably have to expose himself if he crawled out and up the bank to collect his gear and the horse.

Caution would have to be his watchword, at least for a time.

* * *

Upwards of an hour went by. During that time, Cal kept his body submerged and himself from floating away by holding onto reeds. But he grew tired of gripping the reeds, and although the water was warm the sensation of merely floating in it indefinitely irritated him after a time.

His eyes endlessly swept the trees which must have hidden the gunman, but no one showed near the place. Either the killer had gone, or he had great patience. Perhaps he had learned to stalk animals before he stalked men. Such thoughts made Cal shudder. He ran his fingers through his short hair, pushing it back against his scalp. He wondered if Silas would come down to the creek to see what had happened to him after the shooting.

Silas would not come until he had drunk the whole of his bottle of liquor.

The place on the bank nearest to Cal's hiding place was too exposed for a sudden move. He studied the undulating line of the bank further down the creek. He figured that he could take a breath deep enough to see him around the next big patch of reeds and by negotiating them he could reach the shade of a dwarf willow and thus slip clear of the water unobserved. Unless the gunman had made a wide detour from his previous place . . .

Shrugging in the water, he abandoned conjecture and decided to make the move he had thought out, the underwater swim. For a second or so, as he filled his lungs his head came higher out of the water. No bullet sailed towards his head, however, and he made his surface dive and plunged down three feet.

As soon as he could he swam deeper in the water clear of the reeds. Negotiating them was not easy. They were not like moss which undulates and wraps itself around moving objects, but they seemed to exude mud as he scraped past them and that made the visibility bad.

His heart started to thump before he decided that he had arrived in the desired spot. He came to the conclusion that he had been in water too long. He felt the blood thumping through his frame, and he had to expel air before his head came up.

Fortunately, he was under the spread of the willow, and therefore hidden from the other side. His breathing sounded unnaturally heavy to himself as he fought for ease and a greater supply of oxygen. Gradually, his chest subsided to normal, and he was ready to finally leave the turgid waters.

Again he used caution, rolling over the top of the bank almost like a seal. Imitating the action of a newt, he went slowly through the bunch grass, always seeking the longest standing patches for safety's sake.

Fifty yards of progress did a lot to dry him, and he was surprised at the amount of energy it took due to his having to keep his head down. At the end of fifty yards he was perhaps ten yards short of the trees where the gelding had gone foraging, and half as far again from where he had left his clothes. He found himself in a small natural hollow, and there he rested.

He reflected that if his persecutor was still about, and still intent upon killing him, he would be watching the clothes and the horse. More caution. More delay. This time the delay was not so annoying, however, and within a few minutes his head was drooping forward and his eyelids were heavy. He considered still further, and decided that even if he dozed he would become aware of a stealthy approach by the other.

He gave in to his tiredness and slept.

★ ★ ★

When he awoke the sun was well over to the west. Long shadows were gliding across the draw and filling in the spaces between the trees. It was time to go.

Even then, he did not stand up and openly walk across the grass to his belongings. He crept again and felt a slight but nagging new ache in his back due to this unaccustomed mode of travel. His clothes and weapons were just as he had left them. He crawled some more, taking them well within the thin belt of trees before he dressed himself.

He refrained from whistling the gelding, walking a long way after it and only mounting up when he was another fifty yards from the creek. Still following his policy of extreme caution, and at the same time wondering where he had won for himself the patience, he made a further detour and only approached the creek again when the sun was almost down.

As soon as he had crossed the water, he used the trees for further cover, and in the last fifty yards or so before the shack he dismounted again and flitted from tree to tree, well away from the ambling sorrel.

At length, he reached a window and ascertained that Silas was inside, almost in the same position as before. The old fellow had emptied his bottle and dropped it on the floor, before staggering across to the lower bunk and flopping out there in a drunken stupor.

Cal made a circuit of the shack. He did as much reconnaissance as he could, and then stepped inside, flinching unnecessarily. No one else shared the shack with the owner. Now that the ordeal of getting back in one piece was over, the auburn-haired young man began to feel angry. He felt that Silas, however feeble, had set him up for almost certain death, and the old fellow was going to do some explaining before he was left alone to sleep off his drunkenness.

The coffee pot was simmering on the stove when the old fellow received his first shake. Cold water was poured on him from an old cup until at last he opened one bleary eye and regarded his persecutor with a set, angry expression.

'So you're back again, well I didn't ask you to come back an' I'm figurin' on gettin' some rest, so take yourself off to where you came from, mister. You've outstayed your welcome!'

'Not until I've had some explanations from you, amigo! You sent me to a death trap down there at the creek, an' what's more you knew you were doin' it! So rouse yourself, an' tell me why I shouldn't avenge myself on you!'

Cal, feeling most of the anger which he displayed for the old man's benefit, stood him up and hauled him across to the table. He pushed him into the chair and filled his hat with water, sticking it on his head.

In spite of the large quantity of strong liquor, Gallon was beginning to recover. The water almost robbed him of his breath for a time, but he slowly recovered and when he did so, his rheumy eyes followed Cal's every move. He knew about the attack on the young man's life.

Cal lit the lamp which hung over the table and pulled it down to a lower level so that he could see Silas' features while the questioning session was on. They sat facing each other, primed with cups of coffee, and neither of them was at ease.

'All right, so you told me my brother

was in the creek. I figure that for a lie. Somebody told you to send me down there. Somebody wanted me out of the way. Me or anybody else who came along here askin' certain questions! Am I right?'

Gallon hesitated. He glanced around rather fearfully at the windows and then nodded. 'I — I had to do it, but don't ask me any details!'

Silas was almost pleading, but if he expected to be leniently handled by his guest, he was disappointed.

'This is the time for a whole lot of details. Explain what you know, an' don't be coy about it. I still figure my brother is dead an' that you know where he's planted! So talk, Silas!'

Gallon began by shaking his head until he was almost dizzy. 'Why do men have to come lookin' for me in my valley? All I wanted was to be left, to live out the remainder of my days in peace. Now, they've taken my one prized possession.'

His head flopped, but when Cal

cleared his throat it came up again and he did not have to be prompted to go on.

'My coffin. A fine hardwood coffin to take my bones when I'm ready to quit this world. They came along and used it for their own purposes.'

Cal jabbed him on the shoulder with his pointing finger.

'Who are they, and where is the coffin now?' he prompted tersely.

Gallon shrugged. 'Not they, really, only one man.' He opened his mouth to give really worthwhile details, but before he could begin the unexpected happened again for the second time that day. A lethal bullet fired from a heavy calibre shoulder gun came through the window behind the old man and ripped into his back, staying in his chest.

His back arched. The force of the impact threw his body into the table, which would have gone over if Cal had not been on the other side to steady it. Poor Silas fell away backwards and hit the floor, his mouth already frothing, his face showing signs which any ordinary layman would know as the symptoms of impending death.

Rather belatedly, Cal dropped to the floor beside him.

'Who did it, Silas? You've got to tell me now! I'll avenge you if I can!'

Gallon tried to nod, but only succeeded in opening and shutting his glazing eyes. 'In my coffin. Watch out for Forest. *Forest* . . . '

Cal bent closer to catch his last words, but they had already been spoken. 'Forest' he supposed was the name of the killer. He would learn no more from Silas. He figured rightly that the old man had merely been the tool of some killer moving into his territory, and that he had died rather miserably and without any solace purely by ill luck.

Cal lowered his head to the ground and thought about the single heavy shot which had killed the poor fellow. It had not been fired from the same gun which had been used against him at the creek. This one was definitely heavier, might even be a Sharps.

Right now, the owner of the Sharps was either waiting for him to run outside, or he was moving off again. But would he withdraw if he thought Cal had availed himself of important information?

In spite of himself, Cal shuddered. The menace of the afternoon was still out there. He would have to try and tackle it this time. If he didn't he might end his days in Silas' draw.

5

Cal went over the threshold like a snake. He had his Winchester in his right hand and he was ready to put it to his shoulder, but the inky blackness of the first hour after sunset was doing things to his nervous system.

His imagination was over-active. He kept remembering that he had fought with Battling Barnes in a changing room and then Sailor McCardoe in the ring, and that while he had done so, his brother had hurried away towards the Circle S — probably to his death!

And now he had been the close witness to old Silas Gallon's death; a man whose name had been known to him as a child. Silas had put him in a false position at the creek, and now he had inadvertently assisted at Silas' death. Had it not been for the hanging lamp above the old man's head, a killing shot from a distance would have been well-nigh impossible, even for a crack shot.

Silas would have to be planted soon, and by Calvin Simpson, if he survived the present encounter. Troubling thoughts for a man crawling in thick grass near a murder spot. He skirted the shack, and moved slowly through the trees in the direction of the shot. Each tree bole had to be investigated in case it hid an enemy.

His nerves were jumping after the first five minutes. He thought his adversary, whoever he was, had an uncanny way of moving through grass, trees and undergrowth, as well as an eye like an eagle. He mused over the name which Gallon had used. 'Forest,' he had said.

'*In my coffin. Watch out for Forest. Forest . . .*'

After repeating the name, Forest, Silas had gulped in air with difficulty. If he had been trying to say more, he might have been saying *Forester* rather than *Forest*. But that little conundrum could wait. The point was, to locate the gunman now.

Ten yards from the edge of the timber, Cal heard a twig crack. This drew his attention towards the direction of his left hand. He acted on impulse, blasting off a chance shot from his Winchester, and at once rolled into the shelter afforded by the nearest tree.

Seconds later, a bullet from the same weapon which had killed Gallon, hit the wheel of the spur fixed to his left boot. It startled him and took his breath away. The brief flame had shown quite clearly, not to his left, but straight ahead of him and at a greater distance.

It occurred to him for the first time that the elusive gunman with the Sharps carbine might be playing tricks on him. He kept his head down and crawled to the edge of timber. There, he rested. Within a minute a stone hit the bole of the tree above him and further startled him.

Somewhere down the slope beyond the trees a man chuckled airily, as though thoroughly enjoying himself. Cal fired at the sound of the voice and rolled clear of the tree, slowly rolling himself down the slope in an effort to fool the other man.

He pulled up short when another bullet ricochetted off a stone a foot below him on the slope. This time his pores oozed perspiration. But he blasted off two shots with a quick panning of the Winchester in between. He heard nothing to tell him that he had hit his opponent.

This time the return shot did not come. Thoroughly shaken now, he pulled off his spurs and put a substantial dent in the crown of his tall stetson. He tossed the spurs aside and marvelled as one of them jumped on the ground again, hit by a bullet.

Again the gunman cackled to himself. Cal thought he heard a slight scurry of movement. It occurred to him that the other fellow might well be wearing mocassins, so stealthily did he move.

Unnerved by the fellow with the Sharps, Cal recommenced his progress down the slope. This time he moved slower, having an ear for the sounds he made, as well as for the enemy. A premonition that the other was listening hard made him stop his movements about twenty yards short of a shallow gully. His move was timely.

A stone bounced five yards above him, while a second one hit ground rock ten yards beyond. A pity a fellow could not see where a stone came from. Cal moved again, a yard at a time. Some five minutes later, he had reached the rim of the gully. He had long known that this was a dry one, and he was ready to roll into it when two more shots snapped branches off a scrub oak some ten yards further up the bank.

At that moment, Cal resolved to do nothing further to guide the assassin. He would have to be tackled in daylight. Unless the moon decided to show itself. But there was little fear of that. Fortunately, no earth was loosened as he slipped into the arroyo. He crawled along it for a few yards and discovered for himself a cavity in the bank which would give him protection from all directions, except that directly opposite on the other bank.

Rigid self-discipline kept Cal from wriggling about and revealing his hiding place as the killer with the superb night vision silently hunted for him in the next two hours. On two occasions, Cal heard him. The muffled sounds he detected made him certain that the prowler was wearing mocassins.

On the first occasion, he was up the bank in a northerly direction. After standing there without moving for upwards of a quarter of an hour, he moved away again, and reappeared, according to another slight sound, some fifty yards to the south.

Two things disturbed Cal. One was the constant fear that the moon might show, and the second was that the hunter would walk down the bottom of the arroyo and thus be confronted by his quarry curled up in the cavity.

Neither of these things happened. Cal lived with the pain of cramp in his bent legs, and when the pain finally ebbed away he dozed once again. Dawn appeared to take a long time to break that day, and the next half hour dragged interminably as Cal scrutinized the brightening landscape in an effort to be prepared for a dawn attack.

This never came. There was no sign of the assassin anywhere around the shack, the timber or the gully. Cal massaged the aches out of his limbs. He built up the fire in the stove, and moved out to study the ground around the dwelling.

He found the sapling of a scrub pine about half an hour later. There were other saplings of the same type, but this one had freshly turned earth under it and that made it more interesting than all the others. At his age, Silas had not been interested in planting trees.

Fifteen minutes work with a shovel revealed the hardwood coffin which Gallon had babbled about. In spite of the hardness of the wood, someone had cut out on the lid a rough design. It had been done with a sharp knife, and appeared to represent the shape of two or three trees. Cal found himself mouthing the name, Forest.

Perhaps this was the killer's way of leaving his signature on the coffin of one of his victims. It took a lot of nerve for the bareheaded and tense young man to raise the lid of the coffin and learn its secret.

The still face of his brother, Bob, lay revealed to him with a slight fuzz of stubble on the chin. The eyes were closed and the expression was not unusual, which seemed to suggest that death had been instantaneous, before the onset of pain, or even shock. The check shirt and the black vest were tidy, across the front of the chest. The Colt was in its holster, still strapped to the waist, and Bob's Winchester was in the box, alongside of him.

Cal steeled himself to raise the stiff body. He had to take a look at the back. Where the chest was tidy, the back was the opposite. A bullet fired from a heavy shoulder weapon had ripped into the back an inch below the left shoulder blade. Probably a Sharps carbine, fired by a man named Forest, or Forester.

Cal lowered the body back into the coffin. He said one or two prayers over it which he had learned from his father, and then he went back to the shack and removed Gallon's body, draping it across the back of the gelding which had had a peaceful night, undisturbed apparently by the prowler.

Gallon went into the opened grave, but he went in as he was, without the benefit of the coffin. Cal tossed in after him one or two obvious items which he had treasured. He filled the grave in again, and put a crude wooden cross on the top of it, leaving the sapling where it lay, uprooted. He repeated the prayers he knew and then turned his attention to his own needs.

★　★　★

Shortly after five o'clock that same evening, Cal entered the small settlement of North Ford. It was some ten or twelve miles north of the town of Wildcat and nowhere near as significant.

An undertaker with a walrus moustache, who answered to the name of Sam Beard, gave him useful information. The coffin, which had arrived in the town on the back of Gallon's elusive burro, could be sent to the Circle S without delay, provided the Simpsons were prepared to pay well for the privilege.

Chewing on the sides of his moustache, Beard explained that the Town Marshal was out of town visiting a sick relative, and that if Cal wanted to make any sort of a statement affecting his recent doings, he ought to go along to the lawyer's office and talk there.

This led to the office of one Jed Spencer, a mild-mannered lawyer of fifty years. His practice was small, and he lived mostly off the income of his wife, who was the proprietress of a prosperous store.

Spencer offered Cal a comfortable seat and showed a healthy interest in him. The new arrival smoked a cigarette and observed the lawyer before saying why he had gone there. Spencer was a small man with elaborate mutton chop whiskers down his cheeks and very mobile brown eyes and tufted eyebrows.

Cal rose abruptly and walked to a wall, on which was pinned a useful map of the district. He pointed out the approximate location of Silas Gallon's shack and explained that the fellow had been shot the previous day, and was now buried amid his own timber.

Spencer's interest quickened as Cal described the scene and went on to explain his own presence in the district. The Circle S ranch was well known in the district, and also Cal's prowess with his fists. He dismissed his own accomplishments, however, and impressed Spencer with his clarity of mind and his determination to track down his brother's killer.

'The law is not strong in North Ford, Mr Simpson, but you would be well advised to take help in other towns, if you continue to search for your brother's murderer. I sometimes wonder how many honest to goodness Westerners end their days in some remote backwater, the victims of villainy such as you have described as in Gallon's case.

'But tell me, was there anything special about the way you found your brother's body. Any clue as to the type of man who had placed him in there?'

Cal sat back and rubbed out his smoke. He was thoughtful for almost a minute, and then he broke his silence. 'His weapons were there, an' probably his ordinary pocket money, but he lacked two things, now you remind me. The first, of course, was the payroll

80

money which he was carryin' when he was attacked.'

Cal went silent, his mind busy with other details.

'But what was the second thing, my friend? Don't keep me in suspense, I beg of you.'

Cal ran his hand through his hair, and then absently toyed with his hat, which he had retained in his left hand throughout the interview this far. He pushed his right fist into it and straightened it out, restoring it to the undented shape which it had had before he pushed it in the night before, when he was under fire.

'The other item, Mr Spencer, was a hat exactly like this. My brother's colourin' was different from mine. He was fair-headed. But his hat was the twin of mine, right down to the size. So, if you see a man ridin' along with a hat like this one, examine him closely, because there ain't many of them in this part of the territory.'

'They took his hat, as well as the

money. Well, that's worth notin'. It could be a weakness of the killer which might help him to the hangman's noose before he's much older.'

Spencer nodded several times as though to add weight to his latest statement. Cal gave him two dollars for his time, and thanked him for promising to make known to the Town Marshal the facts which Cal had revealed.

The young man sought a hotel shortly afterwards. He retired early, turning over in his mind certain details about the man who had come so near to killing him the previous night.

He was a man who could move like an Indian. He wore mocassins, and was most proficient with two types of shoulder gun; also a knife, judging by the slashed design on the coffin lid. Moreover, he was extremely ruthless and probably quite undisturbed about the men he felt he had to kill.

Understandably, sleep was slow in coming.

6

Hillsburg was larger than North Ford, having a permanent population of nearly five hundred people. It was located north-west of the smaller town and considerably nearer the border with Arizona territory. The hardworked sorrel gelding plodded into the town with its restless young master mounted up almost exactly twenty-four hours after Cal's interview with Lawyer Spencer.

This time he kneed the gelding across Main Street's dust and brought it to a halt by the rail outside the town marshal's office. A wooden notice nailed to the door gave the name of the peace officer as Kit Neal. Cal thought he had heard the name before, but he was not sure.

He secured the gelding and slackened his saddle before going into the office.

While he was busy a leathery face appeared at the office window and grinned at him. The face had a thin blue-black line of moustache trimmed parallel with the smooth brows. A bent deputy's star hung awkwardly from a soiled vest.

'If you want the marshal, he's next door, takin' his food,' the deputy called out.

Cal nodded and glanced at the next building. The window was steamed up, but the smells coming out of it were an excellent advertisement for the food which it sold. The new arrival shrugged. He figured that if the man he wanted to talk to was eating, he might as well eat himself.

A pleasant young woman with the colouring and complexion of a Mexican took his order for ham and eggs, and indicated which of the three other men eating was the marshal.

Kit Neal had a white square of handkerchief tucked into his shirt neck where the string tie was knotted. He was systematically emptying a plate of beef and vegetables as though he had not eaten all day. He was a tall, alert man in his middle forties with thick grey hair and a black moustache. As he reached for his glass of red wine, he noticed Cal's interest and nodded to him.

Cal crossed over and explained that he specially wanted to talk to Neal as soon as the latter was free. While the marshal was agreeing to the interview, Cal's ham and eggs arrived, and Neal gestured for him to eat them at the same table.

Soon, Cal's hunger had abated. Neal was a foot or so back from the table smoking a long thin cheroot and patiently waiting for Cal to get to the same stage.

After smoking a cigarette, Cal agreed to walk the length of the sidewalk with Neal, and to explain the nature of his business. Talking without elaboration, he explained what had happened in Silas Gallon's draw. In much the same way as he had talked to Lawyer

Spencer, he put Marshal Neal further into the picture with regard to recent happenings nearer home.

Some ten minutes later, they squatted on a bench outside a saddler's shop, enjoying the shade.

'So you figure that some hombre named Forest was at the back of your brother's death, an' that the motive was robbery. Am I right this far?'

'Sure, Marshal. That's the way I see it. Why else would anyone want my brother dead?'

'Why else, indeed? But wasn't there something else about the name of Forest you were goin' to explain?'

Cal nodded, while Neal examined the ash on his cheroot. Cal aired again his theory about Gallon's possibly trying to say the name 'Forester.'

Neal nodded and became silent for a while. The bright flickering of his eyes gave some indication of the speed at which his brain worked; other than that, Neal was hard for a stranger to weigh up.

He said at last: 'Forest, or Forester. I'm no stranger to the name of Forester, only I can't see that the Foresters I know have any connection with Circle S affairs, or with old Gallon. You see, the Forester brothers, a scheming ruthless pair of hombres, are in a penitentiary over in Arizona Territory. I ought to know, because along with a lot of other lawmen, I worked to put them there.

'As for the name of Forest, there was a man moved around this county north of here a year or two ago. Name of Forest Jack, or Jack Forest. No one ever seemed to know which way round his name was. He was a good ten years older than the Forester brothers, an' he had quite an unusual background.

'Nobody seemed to know where he originated from, but he was a first class trapper an' something of an expert with a woodman's axe. I heard it said that he didn't fight on any side in the Civil War. Many men I talked with believed that he did a bit of spyin', sometimes for one side an' sometimes for the other. I reckon he lived on his wits, an' when he ran short of supplies he grabbed others where he could from one side or the other.'

Cal sat forward on the bench and showed some enthusiasm for the description of Forest Jack. This sounded like the fellow who had killed Gallon and left the knife picture on Bob's coffin. He said as much, and went on: 'Kit, you mention Forest Jack an' the Forester brothers at the same time. Was there any sort of a connection between them?'

Giving his moustache a twirl, Neal did a lot more thinking.

'You know what? I ain't rightly sure. The memory is vague on the point, but I seem to remember one old timer sayin' that Forest Jack was an older half-brother of the Foresters. I should go along with the idea, but don't take it for gospel.'

'I sure will do that, Marshal, an' now, how about steppin' along to the nearest saloon for a drink on me?'

Neal accepted. They drank together and parted.

* * *

Marshal Neal's talk about the Foresters and Forest Jack spurred Cal on to the next settlement which was a shorter distance than that between North Ford and Hillsburg and almost due west of the latter town.

In its early days this small township had once been called Line, which was not surprising because it was only a little way west of the boundary between New Mexico and Arizona. In the last decade, however, it had dropped its obvious name in favour of another one, Gila Creek, and this second name seemed to have been accepted throughout the county.

This time, Cal took the gelding to the livery and ensured that it had every attention. After slaking his thirst with coffee at an eating house near the west end of town, he entered a barber's saloon for a shave and a haircut. Neither chin nor scalp needed much attention, but he always felt cleaner and fresher after a visit to the barber's.

The barber was a small dark man of Mexican origin with black hollowed eyes. His movements were almost birdlike and his eyes blinked incessantly. Cal nodded to him, picked up an old news sheet and sat himself on a bench.

For a time, the barber talked to the man under his towel, but as replies were few and far between, he grew less talkative, and, if anything, worked even quicker.

The man in the chair had to be shaken when the job was done, as he had fallen into a light sleep. He rose, blowing liquor breath from under his trimmed moustache, and offered the barber a handful of coins from which to choose.

Walking with the slightest of staggers the trimmed man left the establishment and Cal took his place in the seat. The barber shook the towel and tucked it in around his neck.

He said: '*Senor*, I can see that you do not think money spent at the barber's is money thrown away.'

Cal grinned at the little man in the mirror. 'I know what you mean. Some hombres don't visit the barber's until they have hair long enough for a lion's mane.'

The barber chatted on about this and that. Cal relaxed as the soap was massaged into his chin. The razor was moving over his skin with a featherlike touch when the first slight hubbub occurred out of doors. Cal frowned, but stayed relaxed. A door banged not far away, and when the barber changed his position his customer asked a question.

'Hey, what would you say is happenin' out there?'

'A rush of customers for my friend, the liveryman. About four men fresh into town, an' actin' like they could eat the oats for the horses! They've gone in now, but they sure did look impatient by the glimpse I had of them.'

Cal nodded slightly. The trails in that part of the west could make men very dry and very short of patience at times. He wondered who the four men were and where they had journeyed from. Most likely he would never set eyes on them, but they surely were noisy compared with the man Forest Jack, who was still in his thoughts.

The actual shaving was finished and the barber was trimming down Cal's sideburns with a small, neat pair of scissors when the first angry shot echoed round the stalls of the livery and set the horses in there whinneying and kicking the sides of their stalls.

The noise welled up inside the building. Cal sat up and wondered why the shot had been fired. The barber stood further away, watching his reflection and working the scissors on the air. Angry voices came floating along to them. Someone opened the big front door of the livery and a horse came out.

'Maybe I ought to go an' take a look,' Cal murmured tersely. 'I'll be back.'

The barber checked a gesture with his hand that would have indicated that he wanted paying without delay. Instead, he shrugged and held open the door. He had lost customers before through a flurry of gunshots.

Feeling for his gun, Cal stepped out through the door onto the sidewalk. As he did so, two more spirited horses came out through the main door of the livery, held at the head by tired-looking strangers. Fifty yards up the street, a man had gone down on one knee with a rifle to his shoulder.

'You men hold it right there!' he ordered.

One of the craggy featured men holding the horses called for support. 'Hey, Juan, will you drive that hero back into his hole? An' be quick about it! *Muy pronto!*'

'*Muy pronto,*' a shadowy figure on the other sidewalk echoed.

A rifle belched spurts of flame as the

man addressed as Juan fired at the challenger up the street. From another direction, a voice was hoarsely saying that a man was firing on the marshal, so it had to be trouble.

Cal pulled his gun and yelled: 'You over there, hold your fire!'

Almost before he had finished speaking, the two men with the horses opened up with hand guns. The first shot startled Cal, who leapt sideways and luckily avoided shots from the second man, and also from the fellow he had challenged. Juan's gun had been turned on him. To avoid stopping a bullet, he had to do a dive and a forward somersault and a roll into the mouth of the nearest alley.

The leader, a man with red hair and a broken Roman nose, yelled: 'Rudy, will you come on out of there before the whole town turns out?'

A hoarse yell came from the livery. Out through the doors came a tall pale-eyed man on a black stallion. He flicked it with the reins, needled it with his spur wheels and urged it on in a hoarse voice, using cries like those of a rodeo rider. The combined efforts had the desired result. The fellow named Juan had mounted up.

As the quartette surged up the street, kicking up dust, Cal got off a shot at Juan. Again he brought towards him a flurry of bullets, but all of these missed him because he was careful, and also because the departing men were in an all-fired hurry.

A final calculated shot from Cal's Colt hit the last man to emerge. He stiffened in the saddle, but held on and kept going up the street. The distance between the riders and the livery widened. The liveryman, a round-faced individual in faded blue overalls, came out with a gun in one hand. His other hand was pressed to his chest, where a spreading patch of blood showed.

Cal walked clear of his hiding place and fired after the marauders. He felt sure that they had ridden in on clapped out cayuses and stolen others in better fettle to continue their ride. Two shopkeepers emerged also, and they fired weapons up the street. Presently, the town marshal emerged from his alley and sent three rifle shots after the hard-riding quartette, but it seemed clear that they would escape from town with the start they had.

The two shopkeepers stood and flanked Cal, while the town marshal came pacing towards them, his shoulders drooping. He was shaking his head as he said: 'If I didn't know jest where the Forester brothers were, I'd say two of them jaspers were Red an' Morgan Forester, but I must be mistaken 'cause both those boys are in the penitentiary, over the border. So we have new trouble on our hands. How much damage did they do, Jed?'

This remark was aimed at the liveryman, who was still nursing his wound and looked to be in need of instant medical attention.

'They took four good hosses, Marshal. Only the pinto was mine. The other three belonged to my customers.' He shook his head. 'I don't figure they'll be much better than crowbait, unless those jaspers are overtaken real soon.'

'That little breed slipped into my shop and stole forty dollars out of the drawer,' a bald shopkeeper explained. 'Kept a gun on me the whole time.'

'I lost about sixty the same way,' the saddler added.

'Four hosses, an' a hundred dollars. That ain't good. But I'll see if I can raise a few riders, if you like. Really it's a job to give to the sheriff. Nobody ever thanks me for ridin' out of town. Besides, they might jest come ridin' back while I'm away.'

One of the shopkeepers gave a hollow laugh. He had not expected the marshal to do much towards apprehending the wrongdoers. Cal felt annoyed. 'Marshal, when you were assessin' the damage, you didn't mention the wound in the liveryman's chest. Don't that make a posse more necessary?'

'Maybe it does an' maybe it don't. I'll

go down the street an' see if I can raise some help.' He turned about and left them.

The saddler sniffed and brushed his moustache. 'That's Jim Daniel for you. If they'd backed down when he first told them, he'd have fought all right. But when they faced him out he got cold feet. Since he left the Union cavalry, he don't have much time for hoss ridin' or for tanglin' with outlaws.'

The other shopkeeper coughed and spat out. He remarked: 'It ain't only that, Sam. He's spotted the Forester brothers. He knows their calibre, an' you can hardly blame him for not being keen to chase them out of town.'

Cal questioned the shopkeepers and they confirmed that they had seen the Foresters at an earlier date. Apparently they had broken out of the penitentiary. This gave Cal much food for thought. The men he had seen were obviously vicious and quite ruthless but they did not measure up to the image of Forest Jack which he had built up for himself.

7

Marshal Jim Daniel failed to raise a posse. The word had gone around that the Foresters were in the area and that was enough. The Marshal himself rode in a circle around the town, never going further than a mile away. He had with him two deputies, and they were even keener to get back to town than he was when the duty ride was over.

The town was quieter than usual. It seemed to Cal that it was sort of crestfallen because of the way the Foresters had treated it. Marshal Daniel made his rounds of the saloons and other buildings late in the evening. He had a commanding figure, being tall and distinguished-looking with a clear eye and a closely-trimmed greying beard and moustache, but when he had gone by, men shook their heads after his retreating figure.

Cal hesitated about approaching the marshal with his own problems. He decided against it and retired to his room at the hotel with a whole lot of things to think about.

Every few minutes, his conscience queried why he had not ridden out in pursuit of the Foresters, and he had to argue with himself that to take them on single-handed in their present frame of mind was to ask for a quick death.

After a time, he fell into a troubled sleep. The sun was well up in the sky when he roused himself. He moved to the window and looked down into the street. He was in time to see a distinguished looking man arrive on a dappled grey horse.

Cal studied him. He was tall in the saddle, and decked in a smart grey coat and narrow black trousers. A clean dun stetson made him look inches taller, although it was dented at the front. He glanced up at the hotel as he passed and showed Cal a broad face with grey eyes widely spaced in it, and a wide thin mouth. Further down the street he swung the grey horse across towards the marshal's office, but he went on past the office and dismounted outside a coffee house. As he stood on the sidewalk, Cal reckoned he was six feet tall. His hair, revealed when he lifted his hat to mop his brow, was long and dark and parted down the middle. It was brushed back and thick at the nape of his neck.

One other thing Cal had noted about him. He wore a star.

Twenty minutes later, Cal made his way to the coffee house and strode inside. Jim Daniel had partaken of his breakfast at the same table as the newcomer, but he seemed anxious to be finished and back to his work. He was dabbing at his mouth with a white cloth and at the same time pushing back his chair.

'It's good to have you around, Marshal,' he remarked warmly, 'an' let me be the first to wish you luck in the chase after the Forester boys.'

He extended a hand, but the stranger ignored it and went on with his meal. Daniel collided with Cal, and murmured an apology before escaping onto the sidewalk. Cal hovered by the chair which the local man had vacated.

'I'd hate to be a nuisance, mister, but I think I'm in this town for the same reason as you are. I couldn't help overhearin' what Mr Daniel said before he hurried out.'

The seated man plucked a small whisker out of a piece of bacon.

'Are you interested in the Forester brothers?'

'I am. My brother was killed a night or two ago by a man I believe is called Forest Jack. My enquiries seem to suggest that the Forester brothers are Forest Jack's kin.'

'Take a seat, mister. I'm glad to know you,' the visitor said cordially. 'My name is Simon Perry, U.S. Federal Marshal. I came over the border with Arizona in something of a hurry, as soon as I heard the Foresters had slipped out of the pen. You say your brother tangled with Forest Jack? Maybe that old coyote sent the money to bribe the guards for the escape! Jack has enough contacts to have the money smuggled in.'

Cal sank into the chair, suddenly more interested in the talk than in food. He introduced himself and explained how Bob had been relieved of one thousand dollars. Perry ordered for him, and then went on talking in hurried clipped tones.

'Tell me jest what happened when the quartette rode into town, will you? I didn't feel like askin' Daniel because him an' me, we don't altogether see eye to eye about badge totin'.'

Cal grinned briefly and obliged. He put in all the detail he could remember and finished up with a brief description of all four. Perry nodded.

'Yes, those are the boys we're after. Morgan Forester is the older of the two, bein' nearly forty now. He has a cleft chin an' his hooked nose is not broken.

Red is the one who had his nose broken in a fight. Rudy Drax would be the jasper you winged. A tall thin fellow, not much older than yourself, an' with the same colour of hair, too, except that his is thick and coarse. He rolls the brim of his hat, Texas style, an' he has a hoarse voice.

'Number four on this trip is a small fellow named Juan Torres. Half Mexican, half Texan. He wears a round black hat with a stiff brim, like you said in your description, an' he's deadly with all kinds of weapons when he's roused.'

Cal toyed with his food. 'Do you have any idea where they'll head for, or what they'll try to do, Marshall?'

'None whatsoever. The Foresters are unpredictable. They'll raise hell in every way possible, an' no one in their path is safe from a knife or a bullet. They ain't the type of wrongdoer that can be tabulated accordin' to their habits. Havin' said that, I'd say it's too late to expect you might want to ride after them, along with me.'

Cal looked hurt. 'I was jest about to ask you if I could,' he protested.

Perry winked at him and accepted the offer. His last words had not been meant seriously. There was a short silence while they smoked.

Perry broke it. 'Do you have any idea where Forest Jack might be at this time, Cal?'

'None whatsoever, pardner. Why, do you have any clues?'

'All I can think is that Jack fixed their escape, an' that he will be on the lookout for them somewhere in this county.'

'Then maybe we ought to look for Jack first,' Cal suggested.

Perry nodded.

★ ★ ★

Some hours later that same day, the man in question, Forest Jack, was making his way towards the Gila County Lumbering Company up on the timber line of the foothills south of the southernmost spurs of the bulky Rocky Mountains. He was still in New Mexico Territory, but several miles further north than Gila Creek.

Almost ten days had elapsed since Jack rode out of the lumbering camp on his periodic binge. Now, he was returning to the scene of his working life, the pine forest in the foothills. He was a man who had done many jobs and lived many different kinds of life, but lumbering had always interested him, and this was one form of employment he liked to be able to stay with.

He was five-feet seven-inches tall and nearing his fiftieth year of age. His suit was of fringed buckskin. It had kept well on this trip, although he had scarcely worn anything else. A coon-skin cap hid his close-cropped black hair, but his beard and moustache were plain to see, the former being unusually coloured by patches of white hair. A man had once called him a badger and had promptly lost two fingers for his trouble.

Jack's neutral-coloured eyes were bloodshot. He had taken on almost a bottle of good whiskey during the last few hours. The lean buckskin under him showed signs of tiredness, but Jack looked as spritely as ever. His legs were bent around the buckskin's barrel like the jaws of a pair of nutcrackers. Along with his bedroll he had two shoulder guns, a Sharps and a Henry, two .44 Colts and a long knife. All these could be called ordinary weapons, but not so the finely honed axe, his favourite tool as a woodsman.

He checked them over as he rode. His fingers were itchy for something to do, and the mocassined feet in the stirrups also betrayed his restlessness. He felt in his jerkin pocket and produced a Jew's harp, which he examined before placing to his lips. Long before he arrived on the high ground which looked down on the creek and the lumbering company's holdings, Jack's fingers were busily plucking the spring of the mouth harp, sending out jigs and barn dance tunes which carried over quite a distance.

Slowly the buckskin carried him down the slope. Some of the lumbermen working nearest paused in their labours, resting on their axes and peering up the slope towards the new arrival. While he was at a distance, they laughed and talked freely about him, saying what they chose because he was out of earshot, but as he came closer their utterances were more guarded.

Six men came out of the tree felling area led by a huge Swede with the tip of one ear missing.

'Welcome back to the camp, Jack, we missed you. My, my, you must have done well. You had enough money to buy whiskey on the tenth day?'

The other men, Scandinavians, Germans, Frenchmen and less well known nationalities, gathered around the horse and led it forward, all the while looking up at the stocky little man playing the music. When the last sounds of the tune had faded, Jack removed the harp from his teeth and greeted them.

He laughed the skittering laugh which they knew so well. 'Whiskey on the last day,' he repeated. 'You should have been with me. I won a shootin' contest with my Sharps. Enough to keep me away for another week, if I hadn't missed you all this time.'

The Swede smote his chest. 'You hear that, boys, Forest Jack hurried back to see us! I think perhaps he has left behind him some little trouble he wants to forget, eh?'

Jack promptly slipped a mocassined foot out of the stirrup and kicked the Swede on his crumpled ear. 'Don't spend too much time tryin' to figure things out, Swede.'

The rider sounded calm enough, but he was among men who knew him well, men who would take no chances with his hair-trigger temper. No one else attempted any witticisms. Some even wanted to get further away.

8

Half way between the glade where the tree felling was going on and the long log bunkhouse used by the lumberjacks, Olsen, the big Swede slowed the progress of the buckskin and looked up into Jack's face.

'What's it to be, my friend? Are you goin' into the bunkhouse to sleep, or are you goin' to take exercise to sober yourself up?'

The escort of loggers awaited Jack's answer, but none offered any sort of comment in case he turned his unwanted attention on them. He spent almost a minute making up his mind. His eyes were glancing away towards the bunkhouse when a new idea brightened his eyes.

'Tell me, Olsen, have you got any new men on your squad?'

The Swede rubbed his big jaw and

cheekbones. He knew what lay behind this remark, and he could guess what Forest Jack was going to do now. He had to answer the question honestly.

'Sure, there is a new man. He came from Oregon camps, arrived here a week ago. His name is Dowd, Irish Tom Dowd. Have you met him before?'

Jack was shaking his head and looking pleased. Leaning to one side, he plucked the great axe from its sheath and held it up in the rays of the sun. While other heads were upturned to admire it, Jack slipped out of leather. He stripped off his gun belt, but kept his long knife which was attached to the belt which held up his trousers.

'All right, boys, take the buckskin along there. I figure I'll get myself a bit of exercise before I see the inside of the bunkhouse. Show me where the new man is working. This fellow you mentioned, Irish Tom Dowd. I'd like to see him in action.'

Several men exchanged glances behind Jack's back, but they went along with him in order to see the performance which they knew would take place. Irish Tom was just over one hundred yards away, resting his back against the bole of a pine, while a team with horses took away other felled trees.

Like all lumberjacks, Irish Tom was thick in the shoulders and chest. He had spent twenty of his thirty-six years in the United States of America, and lumbering was the job which suited him best. He took a pride in his work, and most men respected him for it.

The top of his head was bald, and, like his face, it was sunburnt and heavily freckled. The fringe of brown hair around his ears and the back of his head looked insignificant compared with his tan. Both his ears were cauliflowered. This suggested that he shared the traditional Irishman's liking for a fight, and that he had not won all his encounters.

As the men walked towards him, Tom straightened up. He grinned at the crowd, waved a hand to them, and then began to frown. There was something unusual about the way they had gathered, something he did not quite understand.

Swede Olsen stepped forward. 'Tom, this is Forest Jack. He's been away on leave ever since you got here, so now is a good time to make his acquaintance.'

Tom nodded and beamed. He stepped forward and extended his hand, but Jack ignored it and gave his full attention to his beloved axe.

'Glad to know you, Jack,' Tom persisted, but again he was ignored. He glanced around, raising his brows in a mute enquiry about the situation. No one answered him. The only looks he received in return seemed to suggest a show of patience.

Jack threw back his head and studied the trees, glancing up to see their silhouettes against the sky. He picked the second out of three. Having made his choice, he unbuttoned his buckskin tunic and allowed it to slip to the ground. He was breathing deeply, causing the muscles of his chest to ripple and grow.

A silence fell around the group of woodsmen. Jack held his axe almost like a baseball bat for a few seconds, and then he swung it. It flashed in the sunlight and bit into the tree. He hauled it out and varied the angle of his attack, sending the first big sliver of wood flying. Working like a machine, he swung again and again.

After about a dozen strokes, his rhythm appeared to falter. He stopped for about ten seconds, gulped in more air and then reapplied himself. This time there was greater power being used. The effects of the alcohol in his blood were dwindling.

Irish Tom stood among the others, his eyes bright and his jaw clamped in a strong line. He admired the polished performance which the newcomer was giving, but the way it had been laid on for his benefit made him angry. It was as if an expert was giving a demonstration for a pure beginner.

Tom's knuckles showed white as he clenched his fists and waited for the tree to fall. Swede was trying to check his rising temper, but Tom would have none of it. A few seconds before anyone else could announce the fall of the tree, Tom filled his lungs and shouted out the traditional warning.

'Timber!'

His lungs were in excellent condition, and the bull-like bellow appeared to affect Jack, whose rhythm varied again. However, the bearded man went on with his work, and in quite a short time the tree creaked, cracked and swayed, and finally fell.

Forest Jack walked to the next tree and put his back against it. Tom strolled across to him. He nodded towards the fallen tree, and the dust which was coming up from it.

'If anyone had told me you were an expert tree feller, I'd have believed them, mister. You didn't have to do that for my benefit.'

Jack eyed Tom, and his expression altered. His eyes slitted and an almost feral look took over. Tom read the obvious hostility, but he declined to do anything about it.

Jack said: 'It's interestin' to meet you, Irish. How would you like to pit your skill as an axeman against mine?'

'I'm earning an honest day's work, amigo, but if you want to show off, who am I to stop you? Fellin' trees is what I'm here for.'

'Take your choice of these other two,' Jack drawled.

Tom grinned, sticking his hands on his hips and studying the faces of the onlookers. It was fortunate that the foreman was down at the creek otherwise there might have been trouble because so many men had stopped working.

The Irishman circled the two trees. While he was on the far side of them, weighing up their girth, Olsen stepped close to him, and whispered in his ear. 'Don't attempt to show up this man,

Tom, it is not good for him to take second best.'

Flaring his nostrils, Tom was about to make a retort about the same applying to himself, but he refrained, and putting on a bold smile he returned to the other side of the trees and pointed to the one of his choice. It was perhaps two inches less than the other one in girth, and seeing that the bearded man intended to try and humiliate him, he felt justified in taking that advantage.

He found that Jack was already standing near the bulkier tree. This rattled Tom, but he did not show it. If Jack expected to win when his task was harder, then he had lots of confidence, and good luck to him.

'Swede, act as judge,' Tom suggested, and this time Forest Jack nodded in agreement.

Tom picked up his axe, studied the keenness of the blade, and pronounced himself satisfied with it. He wondered what sort of an attack to make on his tree. Jack, he figured, would use the short sharp strokes. Perhaps he, Tom, would do better with fewer but stronger strokes of the axe.

Swede said: 'I shall count to three and then signal with my cap. The next signal will mean that the first tree is about to topple. Do you both understand?'

Tom nodded and Jack growled. Ten seconds later, Swede made his signal and the contest started. Men watching held their breath. Tom had worked well while he had been with them, but never as well as he was working now. Back and forth flashed the blade, like a speeding pendulum. Swing, bite, heave, withdraw. And over again. The chips which fell beneath Tom's bole were as big as any of the men ever put out.

Meanwhile, alongside of him, Forest Jack was putting up another remarkable performance. As Tom had guessed, Jack was working with shorter, faster strokes. He swung his blade perhaps four times for every three of Tom's. And yet there was little to pick between their overall performances.

Some two thirds of the way through his bole, Tom's energy began to ebb. He was using up too much muscle power in his wide deliberate swinging. He held on for another few strokes and then stood back, almost lurching as he sucked in air and strove to recharge himself.

Alongside of him, Jack also sprang back, but instead of leaning on his tool, he walked across to Tom's tree and examined it. Letting out a skittering laugh, Jack suddenly swung up his axe and attacked his opponent's tree.

Tom called hoarsely for him to desist, but the bearded man went on until the timber creaked and everyone had to stand aside to avoid the line of its fall. The Irishman walked across to the silent judge and gripped him by the shoulder.

'What do you make of that, Swede? Forest Jack interfered with my work. Are you goin' to name him the winner when it's my tree that fell first?'

One or two of the sightseers risked approving Tom's protest, but most of the men kept silent, knowing that this was a critical time for the Irishman and his hair-trigger tempered opponent. Tom advanced to make his complaint to Jack, but the latter had already stepped away to his own tree. Jack kept his blade working until the second tree fell, and Tom had to run out of the way to avoid being crushed. Eventually, the dust fell and the two contestants came face to face.

Jack looked pleased. Somebody tossed a canteen of water to him and he drank from it. Tom drank from another, and recovered his powers of speech.

'Irish, I did you a favour,' Jack remarked, as he corked up the canteen.

'Some favour, mister. You made me look a complete fool, an' there was no call for that! Maybe you were afraid of losin' in an ordinary contest!'

Jack rested a hand on Swede's shoulder. 'I can see I've annoyed this fellow, Swede. He doesn't know me like the rest of you do. Perhaps I ought to give him a chance to fight for his honour, seein' as how I've acted out of line.'

Swede slowly shook his head. He did not like the way things were shaping up. Moreover, Tom was still angry and in no mood to back off.

'What sort of fightin' did you have in mind, little man?'

Tom was beginning to be rude now. He did not seem to care any more for Jack's reputation. The bearded man did not seem to mind the way he was addressed this time. He reached behind his back and drew from his waist belt the long-bladed knife which was one of his basic weapons.

'Do you think you could handle a tool like this? Well enough to defend yourself, Irish?'

Tom shrugged. 'I'd be better suited with my fists, Jack, but if you've set your mind on usin' the knife, I'll not disappoint you.'

One of the onlookers produced a similar knife. Amid unusual silence, the two contestants wrapped strips of cloth around their left arms and made practice swings with their knives. The blood of one or the other was about to be let. Olsen, who had recently been promoted to chargehand, did not like this development at all. But he knew he could not stop it.

He made sure that the team with the horses was nowhere near, and that the foreman was still busy at some other part of the camp. Then he came back looking pale. He nodded.

'I want you to stop when I tell you to. That will be when one man has wounded the other, or got him in a position from which he can't strike back.'

The eyes of the opponents were on one another. Neither appeared to have heard the Swede's stipulation. Presently, the starting signal was given, and the two hairy chested individuals began to circle one another, holding out their weapons and protected arms like bull-fighters.

Jack moved fast, as always, but Tom had the longer legs and he used them to advantage in attacking and disengaging. After five minutes, Jack had a slight graze on the back of his left hand, while Tom had been nicked over his right collar bone by the very end of Jack's knife.

Neither man seemed troubled by his flesh wound. Another five minutes went by. The spectators were still as quiet, but the breathing of the knife fighters had become noisy. Both men were dripping perspiration now, and their movements were a little more laboured. After twelve minutes, Tom's foot caught a rough patch, but after stumbling he recovered himself and at once went forward.

A minute later, Jack appeared to stumble. He half sank to the ground, moved adroitly backwards, and suddenly lunged at Tom, who had moved after him. Jack feinted with his weapon, then drew it back, and kicked out with a mocassined foot.

The kick was carefully aimed. It caught Tom low in the abdomen, sending pains up through his frame, pains which affected his judgement and made his eyes water. Moaning quietly to himself the Irishman came forward. Jack kicked him again, this time on the knee.

The Irishman lurched. Before he could go down on his knees, Jack moved in close with the speed of a striking rattler. The tip of his knife struck and nicked the skin along the underside of the pectoral muscle on the left side of Tom's chest.

With a slight groan, the Irishman sank to the ground. The crescent wound was by that time oozing blood over the region of his heart. From a kneeling position, the vanquished slipped forward, falling on his chest, head downwards. His chest continued to heave, while the spectators remained for a few moments more as though spellbound.

Clearing his hoarse throat, Olsen stepped forward, waving his arms. 'That's enough!'

The winner, however, ignored him. Jack stepped to the fallen body, and uttered a cry reminiscent of certain Indian tribes at scalping time. On Tom's heaving back, Jack made a pattern with the very tip of his knife. It was crudely done and very lightly drawn, but those who saw it after he had retired were agreed as to what it was supposed to represent. The shape was that of a tree, the trunk and foliage.

★　★　★

The following day, U.S. Federal Marshal Simon Perry and Calvin Simpson were on the trail between Gila Creek and places further north. Cal had remembered something which Marshal Neal of Hillsburg had said in the course of a conversation. Something about Forest Jack being an expert with an axe. Perry had given this some thought and decided that the Gila County Lumbering Company might be a very good starting point in the search for Jack.

Between two and three hours elapsed and the day was at its hottest when the two riders noticed a buckboard approaching them from the north. This trail was the least frequented of any used by Cal since he left home. Travellers had been almost non-existent since they left Gila Creek.

The auburn-headed young man was so interested to learn more about the identity of the buckboard traveller that he pulled out his spyglass and focused it on the conveyance.

'Shucks, Simon,' he remarked, 'this ain't Forest Jack. It's jest an old man in dark clothes an' thick spectacles. He has two mules there pulling him along an' they don't look all that friendly towards one another.'

'Is he showin' any special interest in us?' the marshal asked.

'None at all. I'd say he's very short-sighted an' indifferent to fellow travellers.'

'Maybe you're right,' Perry opined, as the glass was offered to him. 'All the same, we'll endeavour to stop him an' have a little chat.'

Two minutes later, the meeting came about. Perry presented himself at the head of the mules and succeeded in stopping them, although they did not at all like the look of him. Cal rode in close to the buckboard, smiled broadly, and touched his hat.

'Howdy, sir. Do you have a minute or so to spare? My pardner an' I would like to talk to you, if you have.'

Doctor Mike Morris looked very doubtful about chatting with strangers, but his conveyance had stopped. He admitted to being sixty-nine years of age, but he looked older on account of the many small wrinkles in his sunburnt skin. He had stooped for many years, and his suit now fitted him as if it was a size too big.

'What did you want to talk to me about, gents?'

He coughed to clear his throat, and

shifted his position rather impatiently upon the box.

'You're a travellin' gent in these parts. We wondered if you had ever come across a fellow who does carvings with a sharp knife. This may sound like an odd question, but I can assure you it is important to us.'

The doctor gave a sharp intake of breath. 'Young man, that's a strange question. Do you know what business I'm in?'

'Judgin' by the bag you have under the seat I'd say you could be a doctor, sir,' Cal observed shrewdly.

'Right first time, young fellow. Now, when you talked about a man who did carvings, I guess you meant on wood, or some other such substance?'

Cal nodded, and the doctor resumed.

'Well, it jest so happens that I've come across a man who does patterns on the bodies of others. A thoroughly undesirable character, I'd say. I've jest been makin' my weekly visit to the lumber camp, an' this hombre had a fight with another, beat him, an' sketched out a tree on his back with the tip of his knife.'

Perry, hearing this, left the mules and came closer. 'You didn't happen to learn the name of the man who won the contest, did you, Doc?'

The sawbones sniffed and shook his head. 'They wouldn't let me near him. I heard his name, but I've forgotten it. Best I can say is that it reminded me of trees.'

Cal said: 'Forest. Forest Jack, or Jack Forest. Would that be the name?'

'Why, yes, sure, that's it! How in the world did you know?'

'We have business with him, Doc,' Perry explained. 'You've helped us a lot. Have a cigar, will you?'

Morris absently took the cigar, slipping it into his pocket. He was surprised at the speed which the riders used when they resumed their journey.

9

Fifty yards back from the logging basin stood the squarely built timber edifice which was the manager's office.

Around two in the afternoon, Johann Brunner, the manager, was in there alone, pacing the floor and gripping his pipe. He had only been back from a visit downstream about an hour, and he was restless. He had just heard about the clash between Forest Jack and the new hand, Irish Tom Dowd, the previous day.

Brunner was angry. Forest Jack, he realized, was a fine workman, but he was unpredictable. His frequent outbursts of temper always ended up in trouble for one or more of the men. Now, it appeared, the doctor from Gila Creek had complained bitterly about Jack using his knife on Tom's back. The fellow was a menace. He would have to go. Brunner would have dismissed him before this, but he had to find an excuse which would not put Forest Jack into a towering rage.

The shack had more window space than most log cabins. Through the window on the south side, he became aware of a couple of strange riders who looked to be on their way to see him. Brunner groaned. He did not feel like company just then. His woollen logger's cap was on his head, with the ear flaps loose and hanging down. He squeezed it in his hand, tousling his flat, straw-like hair. He gave his closely-trimmed moustache a going over with the back of his hand, and felt in his jacket for his pipe.

As he stoked the pipe, Swede Olsen came out of the bunkhouse and looked baffled. While the chargehand was massaging his face, the two riders drew level with him and addressed a question to him. Olsen answered them and pointed towards the manager's office. The trio came towards it together.

Brunner strolled to the door, sucking hard on his pipe. He showed his head, nodded, and called out: 'Anything special you wanted, Swede?'

The big Scandinavian hesitated. 'Nothin' special, Boss. These gents want to talk to you. I'll come back again.'

Brunner nodded and gestured for the riders to dismount and come indoors. Perry was the first in, and he noted Brunner's eyes on his badge. The Marshal introduced himself and Cal, nodding as Brunner gave his name and occupation.

'I'll come to the point straight away, manager,' Perry promised. 'My pardner an' I are on the trail of a rather tricky customer. Man named Forest Jack. We thought you might have him here.'

Brunner's eyes brightened. 'Was there any special reason you wanted him, Marshal?'

'He's suspected of murder and armed robbery in this county.'

Brunner sighed with satisfaction.

'He's a trouble-maker that one. I'll be glad to have you take him off my hands. Excuse me.'

He stepped to the door and called out to the Swede, who was still within hailing distance. In answer to his question, Olsen replied: 'It was Jack I wanted to see you about, Boss. He seems to have slipped away. Since the fight yesterday, none of the men have wanted to work particularly close to him, an' so we didn't see him go. But he seems to have packed his gear. What shall I do?'

'Which way do you think he'll have gone?' Brunner queried.

'It's hard to say, Boss. You know the way Jack moves as well as I do. But if you asked me to guess, I'd say he crossed the creek.'

Brunner dismissed the Swede and returned to his visitors, who took the news with obvious disappointment.

★　★　★

About the same time that Cal and Perry were receiving the message from Brunner, Forest Jack was in an isolated log cabin a mile and a half away on the other side of the creek. For upwards of a year the building had not been used by the outfit, owing to the fact that the nearby timber had been thinned out and left rather denuded.

Jack was in good form. His half brothers, Red and Morgan, and their two sidekicks, Drax and Torres, had only arrived there in the last hour. The brothers had served about half of a stiff sentence for armed robbery, and this coming together again was something of an event for them.

Jack had a stock of food in the place. He had shown another of his skills when he produced a hot meal in a very short space of time.

As soon as the four edgy men had filled themselves and washed down their food with good coffee, Jack produced a hidden stock of clothing and invited them to throw away their old gear in favour of the new. Drax and Torres were as eager as the others to help themselves to the new outfits, but they held back, knowing the uncertain temper of their host.

Jack paraded his kin in front of the mirrors, drawing grudging admiration from them for the work that he had put into this meeting.

'All right, so who would guess now that you'd been in the pen, boys? Nobody, I'd say. You look too prosperous. Let me give you a shave and a haircut, then you'll look like millionaires!'

Red tossed some of the spare gear in Drax's direction. He turned to his brother, and Morgan grudgingly admitted that he could really do with a shave and haircut. Jack produced the knife with which he had marked Irish Tom, but Morgan was not having that used on his head.

'A proper razor, scissors, or nothin' at all. You hear me, Jack?'

The older man nodded and dropped

his fooling. He put a towel round Morgan's neck and began to apply the soap. All the time he worked, he whistled, as he did not have a hand free to work his mouth harp. In fifteen minutes, Morgan had been transformed and Red was in the chair.

As the razor moved over his face, Red frowned. 'Jack, you ain't said much about Larry. What did he say when you made contact with him?'

'That's a good question, boy, one you should have asked before now. Larry was well established. I taxed him about becomin' active again, an' he said he wasn't ready. He's on this big spread, see? The Circle S they call it. An' I figured he was playin' a waitin' game, tryin' to get in on the management. Anyway, I figured to let him stay that way for a while. Long enough for me to have you two sprung out of jail. It's up to you an' Morgan what we do about Larry. You've always known that.'

Jack, Red and Morgan chatted on about old times, times when the three of them and Larry Raybold had ridden together. Before the days when the brothers had been apprehended and put away.

Morgan was saying some pretty unkind things about how easy Larry had been living when an unusual expression flitted across Jack's face. He held up his hand for silence, and the others at once stopped talking. The grooming was over, so the old timer was able to cross to the door in a hurry and listen. For a few seconds, he hesitated.

Morgan brought him back to the present. 'All right, what does it mean? I heard it!'

Red also glowered at Jack's back. 'Spill it, will you, Jack? That owl hoot, it was a message of some sort. You wouldn't hold out on us at a time like this, would you?'

Jack turned slowly to face them. 'After all the trouble I've taken to get you out of the pen an' up here? Of course I wouldn't. We're kin, ain't we?

Only that message was a warnin'. I still have a few friends back there in the camp. It means somebody's on my trail. We'll have to pull out, in a hurry!'

Red and Morgan were on their feet. They cursed Jack quite roundly, being the only men alive who could hand out that sort of treatment to Jack and get away with it.

'Maybe your plannin' ain't all that good, brother,' Red remarked heavily. 'Could be you've brought the law along with you. Are you losin' your touch?'

Jack gestured at them with his hands, while Drax and Torres looked on, not quite knowing what to do about this family row.

'Now hold on, boys, be fair now. After all, you four made a strike in a town not far from here. You might have brought along the law, not me!'

For a few seconds everyone seemed to be shouting at once, and then the gravity of the situation sobered them.

'All right, then,' Jack offered, 'I'll take the blame. The trouble is comin' from the other side. You boys ride on, make your getaway. Me, I'll hold back an' shoot the trouble off your tail. How will that be?'

'But you'll be comin' with us, Jack?' Drax queried unexpectedly.

'Nope, I don't think so. I like lumberin' an' I don't want to give it up altogether. I'll stay, keep out of sight, then, if all's well, I'll go back to tree-fellin' for a time. It'll work out. You'll see!'

The brothers studied Jack for a moment as he examined his Sharps and other weapons.

Morgan suddenly became anxious. 'All right, boys, get your things together. We ain't in any special danger, but it don't do to give the opposition too much time to come up with us. Jack knows what he's doin'. I guess he'll find us again when he's good an' ready.'

Five minutes later, the four were mounted up and ready to ride off again. Each of them stared with interest at the figure of Jack, who had elected to be their rear guard. They wondered if he would succeed in killing the opposition and in keeping out of harm's way for himself.

Jack watched them go like a doting father parting from his youngsters. As the trees swallowed them, his expression changed. He began to load his various weapons onto the buckskin. It was time to be away. Already his active brain was busy with plans for the coming ambush.

10

Johann Brunner was no coward. He had to be dissuaded from crossing the creek with the two visiting riders who were seeking Forest Jack. He stayed behind with an ill grace, although he knew that their advice was good. The lumbering enterprise would cease to function if anything happened to him.

As they emerged on the other side of the creek the riding partners discussed the manager. It made a change from troubled thoughts about Forest Jack and his blood relations.

The sorrel gelding and the dapple grey were now used to each other's company. They moved on through the rich growth of trees, matching stride for stride, and enjoying the leafy overhead. A mile further on the trees were visibly thinning.

Although they did not show it the

partners began to feel anxious. They glanced at one another and nodded. The critical time was near.

'Any special precautions we ought to take?' Cal queried.

He checked the pace of the gelding. The grey automatically did the same. Perry was rubbing his nose. He had a feeling of foreboding, but there seemed to be little he could do about it.

'The shack will show up presently. It shouldn't be hard to find. Let's stop at the edge of the trees an' discuss the situation then. After all, we didn't know that the old jasper is expectin' us. He took off because he wanted to, not because we were close behind him.'

Cal gave a wry smile. 'The last thing I expect is for Forest Jack to surrender himself into our hands, Simon. I think we'll have trouble, one way or another.'

Perry nodded, rather gloomily. A minute later, he pointed forward, indicating the wooden shack about a hundred yards or more ahead.

'Look out for any sort of movement

now, in case the old rascal tries to take us by surprise. He's capable of anything, judgin' by that awful night when he nearly eliminated you!'

Cal was thinking about the Sharps carbine when the shot rang out. It came from a good distance, but was not exceptionally far away. The bullet was aimed at Simon. It came from trees many yards to one side of the shack, which was then empty.

Cal and the gelding stepped sideways, the rider glancing towards the direction of the attack. The dapple grey horse also stepped sideways, but for a different reason. The bullet had hit the animal in a vital spot in the body. Perry had survived the surprise attack. A few inches variation in aim would have killed him.

Only seconds were needed for the alert riders to take some action. Cal crouched low and pulled out his Winchester, while the dying grey slipped to the ground under its startled master. The sorrel, released of its burden, turned around the way it had come and trotted off to a safer distance.

Bellied down behind adjacent trees, Cal and Simon caught their breath and stared in the direction of the marksman.

'What do you make of that, amigo?' Perry asked.

'It's the sort of thing I could have expected of Forest Jack, but for some reason he didn't use the Sharps. Had he done so, I think you might have been wounded.'

'Not wounded, dead! Don't bother to spare my feelings, Cal. You were right. We should have taken precautions earlier. Now I've got no hoss. An' we could be in some danger. We'll have to move about a bit, or else we won't find out the strength of the opposition.'

Cal had a feeling that it was definitely Jack shooting, and that he would be on his own. Neither of the friends had any reason to believe that others of the same clan had been at the shack just recently.

Perry's simple strategy was put into practice. With ten to fifteen yards between them, the two men moved through the thinned trees towards the rear of the shack and trouble.

Their opponent permitted them to cover some fifty yards and then he opened up again. Cal parted with his fine stetson. He pulled it back with the barrel of his Winchester and pushed in the top to make it less of a target.

While Perry was crawling forward he received a bullet hole in his right sleeve. He was fortunate that the skin of his arm was not burned. Cal had fired at the gun flash, but failed to hit the mark.

Progress was slow, but it would achieve something, if they were lucky enough to remain unhurt. Whoever was shooting at them would have to move his position, if he was not to be caught between two guns.

★   ★   ★

Cal and Perry were moving roughly towards the north.

Beyond the denuded area to the east, the four men who had broken out of the penitentiary were also considering the situation. They were mounted up, but well hidden by screening foliage and shadow.

Red was saying: 'Why in tarnation don't he use that Sharps? The old goat could have killed the marshal an' maybe the other fellow as well by now, if he'd only used his best weapon!'

Morgan Forester continued to regard the distant situation through a spyglass. Drax was anxious to put distance between themselves and the scene of the shooting. Torres, for once, had an opinion to offer.

'I think I know why Jack does not use the Sharps. He does not want anyone to know that it is he who is firin' against the peace officer. You will recollect that he wanted to go back to the camp and work there after the prowlers have gone.'

Red fingered his broken nose. He turned to Torres, nodding slowly and lifting his brows a little in brief admiration.

'You know, Morgan, Juan could be right, at that! Can you see anybody comin' from the other side of the creek?'

'Nope. Nobody at all. Are you figurin' on givin' Jack a helpin' hand?'

'Well, we ain't doin' him or us any good here, jest sittin' watchin'. So why we don't go back there an' hit those two lawmen on the flank?'

Morgan at once approved the idea. Drax would have argued against it, but he knew that to be in a minority of one was not healthy in this company. Keeping within the fringe of trees, the four riders rode around the denuded area from the east, coming up behind the other two from the south-west.

Leaving their horses all tied to the same bush, they took their weapons with them and availed themselves of all available cover. By that time, Jack was flitting from tree to tree, but his movements — unpredictable like everything else about him — made a snapshot difficult, and so he remained unscathed. Ten minutes after they dismounted, the quartette were getting within rifle shooting distance. Morgan made signs for them to hold their fire for a while, and he hastened still more, confident that the men they were stalking would not look back.

Jack fired his Henry from behind a tree. At once he rolled sideways and discharged it again from behind a different bole. A bullet from the marshal's rifle went within an inch of him. He nodded solemnly as though acknowledging a good effort.

For two or three minutes now, he had a feeling that others were about to take a part in the hunt. He had seen no movement from the west, where the creek and the main part of the camp was located, and he was confident that the newcomers were on his side. His spirits brightened considerably. The only people likely to take up arms on his behalf were his half brothers and their allies. If they were about to help, it meant that they had regretted the harsh words spoken against him in the logging shack.

He could have cheered, except that it would have done his situation no good at that stage. If the boys were with him, all well and good. If he had misread the situation, then he would use the Sharps to shoot these two persistent peace officers off his back, regardless of the consequences.

No sooner had he come to this decision than four rifles all sounded off at once. The gunmen were well spread, with anything up to fifty yards spanning their cautious approach. After the first burst, they fired one at a time, causing consternation up ahead.

One bullet nicked Perry's boot. Others plucked at Cal's bandanna and holed the back of his vest. It was a time for really grovelling close to the earth and hoping for the best. The bullets continued to fly, all fired by the four men in the rear.

Pinned down and without any serious hope, the two men under fire wondered what they could do to better their position. The slightest move on their part would draw bullets from the rear, and if they were not very careful, they would present a target to the man up ahead of them.

'What next, Simon?' Cal called out anxiously.

'Wait a short while longer, then put up one or two shots for Jack's benefit. After that, we'll have to make a move, slightly nearer to Jack, if it is him up there! We can't afford to stay here, or we'll be blasted from the rear!'

'Those are my feelings exactly,' Cal replied.

He sniffed, and parted grass with his nose as he peered past the roots of a tree in the general direction of the man ahead.

Morgan Forester held up his hand a mere inch or two and halted the forward movements of his squad.

'I think we're near enough for us to make a short run apiece, covered by the other guns. I'll take the first go. Wait till I give the signal!'

Red grunted his approval, but the signal was long in coming, because the two men caught in the pincers at that moment both fired ahead of them at their original quarry.

'They're goin' to make a run for it, I think,' Red murmured. 'Let's be ready for them!'

Drax muttered something in his excitement. Torres was slowly moving the tip of his tongue around his dry lips.

Suddenly Morgan called: 'Hold it!'

Marshal Perry moved up five yards and dived into cover, avoiding a bullet from Jack, and Red turned to curse his brother, his face convulsed.

'Why in tarnation did you do that, Morg?'

'Riders comin' in from the creek side!' Morgan murmured rather tersely.

The others' heads swivelled around, but they saw nothing. Torres applied his ear to the ground and in seconds he was nodding in agreement with Morgan. 'Three or four horses, at least, amigos. Maybe it is time for us to move our position, no?'

Morgan growled with anger, and Red fought to control his temper. For a few seconds their eye glances came together. Prudence was something they scarcely ever bothered about, but they had been on the run for so long that they did not want to be apprehended in these woods. Not when they had simply stayed behind to do Jack a favour.

Fear made Drax bold. 'Jack can slip away on his own. He's the best man I know in timbered country. Maybe we ought to make tracks now, seein' as how we don't know the strength of the opposition!'

'I don't like agreein' with you, Rudy, but for once you're right,' Red admitted grimly.

He nodded his head in the direction of their horses and his partners started to pull out right away. No more shots were fired by them, and the withdrawal was a much speedier affair than their approach. Cal and Perry stayed down and only moved when they felt they had a reasonable chance, but after some five or six minutes they began to feel some slight confidence that the four at their rear had pulled out.

Cal kept his eyes on the small cluster of trees where he thought Jack was, but he talked at the same time. 'If they've pulled out when they had us pinned, what can it mean?'

'It can only mean one thing. They know something that we don't. Everybody over at that loggin' camp across the creek must know there is shootin' over here. Maybe some of them are beginning to grow a little curious.'

Cal had hoped that help might be on the way. At the first suggestion of confirmation, some of the fire went out of him. Shooting at others, and being shot at oneself was always something of a strain.

Further relief came when Perry whispered that he could hear horses. The firing died out altogether. Perry tied a kerchief to his gun stock and held it up, making sure that their enemy could not see it. Cal's eyes never left the supposed position of their quarry.

Presently, Brunner, who was using a glass, spotted the signal. He pointed it out to the two sheriff's deputies who had arrived from the county seat to look for the Foresters. The trio came forward with caution. No gun challenged their right to be there.

When it was established that all the hostile gunmen had left the scene, a search was made of the area. Apart from a few discarded items in the cabin, only a few horseshoe prints and empty shells told of the recent encounter.

11

For two days a posse from the county seat hunted the Forester brothers in the open. Their mission kept them active for twenty hours out of twenty-four, but although they kept the redoubtable brothers and their sidekicks on the move, they did not catch up with them.

While the posse was busy looking for the quartette, Cal and Marshal Perry spent some time in hunting for Forest Jack. Perhaps it was fortunate that he had decided to put a useful distance between the logging area and himself, as he would have proved a fearful menace to the pair of them, if they had come upon him during the hours of darkness.

These two gave up the search before the posse did, and, after some discussion, they backtracked towards Gila Creek. In order not to advertise their presence, they parted company before going into the small town, and agreed to stay apart for a while unless any special development occurred.

★ ★ ★

On the third day of the hunt, the Foresters and their partners were beginning to tire of constant motion. They went to earth in the afternoon in a circle of rocks just north of the trail between Gila Creek and the county seat, which was away to the east.

Morgan coughed as smoke from their fire was blown into his face by a light breeze. 'This far we've been lucky. We made a good selection when we grabbed these hosses an' they haven't let us down. They need a rest, an' we need a change. Anybody got any ideas?'

For once, Red had nothing to say. He was in a morose mood. Although he made no mention of his thoughts, he kept wondering how Jack had made out, after they left him to fight alone.

Juan Torres got up and strolled away, a spyglass under his arm. Drax, faced with Morgan's probing glance, dropped his eyes to his clothes. The hat with the broken brim had been discarded in favour of a new dun stetson. He had taken some pains to roll the brim to a point at the front. Previously he had never worn a coat on expeditions of this sort, but the one which Jack had provided pleased him. It was cut out of good grey cloth by a tailor who knew his business. Drax was proud of it.

He glanced at the other two. Red had a brown corduroy coat and a stetson of the same colour. Morgan's jacket was of fine black cloth, matching his tall dented hat. All three of them looked different. Only Torres, perched on a rock with the glass to his eye, did not seem to have been transformed by Jack's offerings. Jack had given him a big-crowned undented stetson, but he had kept to his flat black hat with the straight brim. The stetson had gone into his saddle bag.

'Well, Rudy?' Morgan prompted. 'You're lookin' thoughtful. What do you have in mind?' Before Drax could answer, Torres called: 'There is a vehicle comin' this way from the county seat. It could be a stagecoach!'

'I was about to say these clothes could help us to change ourselves a little. How would it be if we made out to be coach travellers, for instance? If we brushed ourselves down, we might move into town unnoticed. We could clean up in the night an' be on our way again before daybreak. What do you think?'

Morgan said: 'It's an idea, an' we're short of them right now.'

Torres came hurrying back. 'It's a coach, all right. Judgin' by the way it's rockin' about, I'd say there aren't many passengers in it. Perhaps it's late, also.'

Red outlined briefly what Drax had suggested. Torres was mildly enthusiastic. 'It would give the horses a rest, an' if I can judge distance, it will be dark when the coach reaches town. It must be late on schedule.'

'We'll give it a go,' Morgan decided. 'Give yourselves a good dustin' down, boys, an' turn on the charm. We'll let Rudy here do the talkin' in the first place. He used to be a salesman. He'll know what to say.'

Five minutes later the coach topped the gradient nearest to their position and for the first time the crew up on the box knew they had company. The flinty-eyed driver gave them a chill look when he saw their numbers, and their mounts.

Rudy Drax edged his stallion forward. 'Howdy, gents, we don't want to upset your routine at all, but we were wonderin' if you had any room inside. The fact is, we've been doin' a little surveyin' in the lumber region an' we're slightly off our bearings. We wondered if we could travel into town with you, so as to give our horses a rest.'

With his unruly hair and sideburns trimmed down, Drax looked quite presentable. He glanced up at the shotgun guard, who looked anything but pleased at the delay.

'Boys, it's like this. We're behind schedule, an' our passengers might not take kindly to your numbers.'

'Maybe if I spoke to them,' Drax suggested.

An elderly man and woman had already put their heads through the windows on the near side, the better to see who had stopped the coach. Drax moved along to speak to the man. The male traveller was around sixty in age, with a firm mouth and chin and sagging cheeks. His eyes were pale, but shrewd looking. He rested his hands on the top of an ivory handled walking stick. A tall silk hat covered his white hair, and a cloak of dark material covered most of his bulky figure.

His wife was a demure little person in a dark billowing gown. She had on a short coat and a broad straw hat, tied under the chin with ribbon. An opened book lay on her lap.

'Good day, sir, madam, I wonder if

you would agree to have with you four riders who need a rest from the saddle?'

'By all means,' the traveller replied. He gestured towards his wife, who nodded graciously. They gathered up their simple belongings and moved into one half of the rear seat. A further consultation took place between the riders and the crew, and then the horses were tied to the boot.

As soon as they were aboard, the vehicle rolled. Drax introduced each of his partners, giving fictitious names. The elderly male passenger informed them that he was Henry Ainly, an English writer. The Ainlys were travelling the west looking for copy for a novel.

One after another, the non-talkative outlaws pretended to nod off to sleep. Drax kept up a conversation for a quarter of an hour. After that, he showed signs of sleepiness, and Mrs Ainly chided her husband for prolonging the conversation.

★ ★ ★

Shortly after dusk, the coach entered Gila Creek and moved up the main thoroughfare, stopped outside Creek Hotel. Morgan was the first out. He kept his eyes away from the two or three men who showed an interest in the coach, devoting a little effort to helping Mrs Ainly out of her seat. Red and Rudy helped with the old couple's luggage and the first scrutiny was soon over.

A man went away with the mail sack, and the porter from the hotel took in the Ainlys' hand luggage. Red and Juan attended to the horses, while Morgan gave the front of the hotel a close scrutiny, and beckoned Drax forward to do the talking at the desk.

Out came the porter again, anxious for another tip. 'You gents goin' along to the livery before you book in?'

'Tell me, do you have any sort of open space behind the hotel where we could leave the horses for tonight? We don't want to bother puttin' them in stalls.'

'If you like I could take them along for you.' Morgan's frown checked this offer. 'There is a small corral at the back an' some straw an' grass. It ain't often used, that's all.'

Red and Torres took the horses up the passage and round the back, and Morgan nudged Drax along in front of him. 'Deal with the register. If the old couple are still about, remember the names you gave us in the coach.'

Necessity brought Drax back to wakefulness. He signed in for all four of them. They had been allocated two double rooms on the rear corridor, first floor. Morgan waited for him at the turn in the stairs, and the other two followed them up almost at once.

They spent the first half hour freshening up, and then sent the porter out to get them some food from the nearest eating house. It came in fresh and steaming and reminded them that they had not eaten many specially

163

prepared meals of late. While they ate their minds were busy and the plans began to formulate.

Red started things off. 'We can't expect to stay in this town any length of time unrecognized. So we get together as much dinero as we can durin' the dark hours and then we hightail it out again, without givin' ourselves away, if that's possible.'

'Where do we look for the money?' the 'breed asked.

'Right here in this hotel,' Morgan explained. 'Every room bar these two an' number six.'

Drax's brows went up in enquiry.

'Leavin' out the Ainlys,' Red replied. He was superstitious about such things as robbing fellow travellers, rather than sentimental.

'If we're goin' to get out without a fuss, it'll mean bein' very light on the feet,' Red resumed. 'Either that, or a lot of victims will have to be trussed. Me, I don't feel like ridin' out of this burg with a whole pack of riders at my heels.

So we'll take no chances.'

The discussion went on a little longer. When all four were satisfied as to their assignments, they stretched out on the beds and the floor and smoked. One room would have done for all four of them, except that it might have made someone suspicious.

★ ★ ★

At midnight, the whole town was quiet. Peace officers had made the rounds and the last of the honky-tonk pianos had given out its last tune. Lamps were dimmed along Main Street. Only the moon gave a ghostly glimmer and that made little difference.

Rudy Drax was the first on the move. He had been given the job of rounding up the horses and making sure that they were ready for a speedy getaway. He came down the stairs with his boots in his hand, and sighed with relief when he found the foyer empty.

One dimmed lamp helped him to

pick his way to the entrance where he pulled on his boots and stepped out into the open air. Anyone seeing him now would have reason to be suspicious, so he took every precaution in staying out of sight. No one was in sight, either way.

He stepped into the alleyway and tiptoed round the back, taking long careful strides.

Torres started on the ground floor rooms which were at the back of the building. He succeeded in entering and leaving the room of a middle-aged couple without disturbing them. He came out with a wallet and a handbag. He was entering the next room when it occurred to him what risks he was taking. One unexpected scream would send up the alarm and put their liberty in jeopardy.

After that, he used the bedding to gag and tie his victims. It made the job a good deal slower and the passing of time played on the nerves. Fifteen minutes later, Red and Morgan had just about finished the upper floor. They met outside number six and reminded each other that the Ainlys were in there.

Morgan whispered that he was going below to check how Torres and Drax were getting on. Red nodded and opened the door of number five. Fortunately for them, several of the fourteen room occupiers did not lock their doors, and those who did took their keys out of the doors.

Either one or other of the two keys issued to the quartette fitted every locked door. Number five opened easily. Red stepped through it and closed it behind him. He, it was, who had given out the instructions for making the individual robberies. Now, he was getting tired of the routine.

As he waited behind the door, the fellow in the single bed turned over, as if he were aroused. Red stepped close and hit him behind the ear with the butt of a revolver. The sleeper groaned and stayed very still. It was as well that he did so, because the broken-nosed intruder had a knife ready to silence him forever.

The man in the bed gave no more trouble. Red was looking around for his belongings when the sound of snoring through the wall suddenly ceased. A familiar voice called out: 'Henry! Henry! Do wake up, all is not well in this hotel! You know how accurate I am over these things. Get up and do something. Ring a bell, or something. Do you hear me?'

There was the sound of muttering as the disturbed sleeper was aroused. The woman was not satisfied. Filling her lungs she called out at the top of her voice. 'Help! Manager, porter! Anybody! Turn up the lamps at once! All is not well!'

Henry Ainly got out of bed and sounded to be dressing. He acknowledged his wife's distress and assured her that he would rouse the other patrons. Red cursed them both and decided that it was time to leave the building. The Ainly woman would be the downfall of them if they didn't hurry.

He stepped out of the door again, closed it silently and hurried down the carpeted steps with his boots slung round his shoulder. Not many people had emerged from their rooms as a result of the shouting from number six, but through an alcove downstairs the staff of the hotel were beginning to tumble out.

Red whistled and stepped out into the open air, hurriedly looking both ways. The heavy steps of his brother, coming from the rear of the ground floor, gave him some reassurance. They called out for Torres, who appeared a moment later struggling to get his second boot on.

'Let's hit leather,' Red suggested.

The four horses were tethered to the rail in front of the hotel, showing that Drax had done his job properly, but of the tall outlaw there was no sign at that time.

★ ★ ★

The occupant of number five, who happened to be Cal Simpson, was tipping cold water over his head from a ewer as he heard the altercations going on down below. His window was open and the room overlooked the street. The blow with the revolver had not been as effective as Red had thought. Apart from a stinging pain, and a promise of a useful bruise Cal had not suffered very much.

'Where in tarnation is that fool, Rudy?'

Now he knew beyond doubt that the Foresters had made another daring raid. Only luck had kept him still after the blow from the revolver butt. He had not known about the knife. And here was a chance to get off a few hostile shots, if he hurried.

He put the jug aside and grabbed for his gun belt. Blinking water from his eyes, he catfooted round the room, only to hear the sound of horses being put to the gallop. He leaned out of the window and saw that one horse was still at the rail. Of its owner there was no sign, but as long as it was there Cal stood a chance of picking him off. A man shouted, well up the street. A bleary-eyed hotel attendant blundered into the foyer half-dressed.

Cal stuck his gun in the air and fired off three bullets. The sound of the shots reverberated up and down the empty street, bringing cries of alarm.

Quite unexpectedly, a shop door opened under the sidewalk awning opposite. Rudy Drax came out with a bag tucked under his arm. He looked around him and ran obliquely across the dirt of the road, heading for his mount, the black stallion.

Cal got him in his sights, panned his gun carefully and cut him down with two well aimed bullets. Drax's legs stopped working. He sank into the dust and his new hat rolled away. When the first running men came along, the outlaw was dead.

One of the runners recognized the stallion as his own stolen property. He pumped an extra shell into the outlaw's corpse for good measure.

12

Needless to say, the town of Gila Creek was a long time settling down after the precipitate departure of the Forester brothers and Juan Torres. Upwards of a score of men came along with lamps, anxious to have a close look at the face of the dead man. While they were busy with the details of this sensation, the doctor was sent for to attend to those with chafed limbs due to the ropes and bedding which had bound them.

No one suggested a chase after the three runaways by night. It would have been foolhardy, in any case. The incident brought Simon Perry from his lodgings up the other end of the town for a consultation with Cal. They decided at that time that nothing further could be gained in Gila by pretending that they were not working together as partners.

For the apprehension of Drax, on the run from the penitentiary and shot while compounding another felony, Cal was due a reward. An application had to be made to the proper authority and time would be taken before the money came through. The partners discussed their future moves with several of the townsfolk, including the man who had recovered his stallion, and Jed, the wounded liveryman.

Perry explained that he needed a good horse to make up for the one shot from under him. The listeners, who were grateful to Cal for bringing down Drax and saving another shopkeeper's hard-earned dollars, decided that Perry should be offered the black stallion recovered from the dead man.

When the reward money came through, it could be used to compensate the real owner of the stallion and others who had lost their horses at the same time.

Cal beamed as he heard this suggestion. He called for a round of drinks for all concerned, and the men in the saloon drank to the downfall of the Foresters and their confederates.

★ ★ ★

Around eight o'clock the following morning, Cal and Perry rode out of town, taking the easterly route. There were many people to see them go and to wish them well. They exchanged greetings with a few, including the Ainlys, who had been so close to the outlaws, and who were enthusing about the fascinating material they had collected for their book.

Sorrel and black settled down to an easy pace which suited their riders for the first hour or so.

Cal was thoughtful, which led to conversation. 'We're goin' east, pardner. I think it's the right direction, but I'm not sure why.'

'They wouldn't be fools enough to double back north, anywhere near the lumbering outfit. If they recross the

175

border they're likely to be picked up and put away again. That leaves the east an' the south. If we don't get an inklin' of where they've gone soon, I'm goin' to suggest we turn south.'

'Okay, so there must be a theory behind your reasonin'. If we go south, where do we head for?'

Perry delayed his answer for almost a minute. 'Somewhere nearer the Circle S.'

Cal whistled. He started to rethink the whole business. Why had Forest Jack been so close to Circle S territory when he shot Bob Simpson? Why was he that far south of the lumbering camp, and the place where his half brothers crossed the border?

Cal voiced these questions, and found that Simon was just as interested in the answers to them.

'A man who is as mobile as Forest Jack wouldn't go all those miles jest to jump a ranch payroll. He could have struck at some place much nearer Gila Creek.'

'Unless he had some special reason for bein' there. Some contact,' Cal reasoned.

'Somebody who knew exactly when to expect the ranch payroll would be passin' a certain place.'

Cal scowled, he was thinking so hard. 'Someone in town, or someone at the Circle S.' He whistled again, as another consideration occurred to him. 'Say, Simon, I'd like to think that somebody deliberately arranged it that I wouldn't arrive on time to escort my brother with the payroll.'

Perry nodded. 'If it ain't too painful for you now, tell me again all that happened after you reached town on the day your brother disappeared.'

Cal did so. He talked for upwards of half an hour. When he had finished, Perry asked a few questions and then brooded over the answers. Eventually, Cal pressed him for his conclusions, and Perry gave them.

'Somebody in Wildcat, or on your father's ranch, might very well have arranged for that Tillot fellow to distract you from your main purpose on that special day. I don't suppose you'll have any ideas yet who it might be, but you'll have lots of time to work it out before we finish this hunt.'

Cal nodded in agreement. The riding went on, through the morning and the afternoon, except for an hour off in the heat of the day. Early in the evening, they encountered a posse coming away from the next town, Hillsburg.

From the sheriff's men they learned that nothing had been seen or heard of the three surviving outlaws near the town. After exchanging news, they parted again, the posse to work the terrain further east, in the direction of the county seat.

Cal and Simon had turned south by the time they started looking for a night camping site.

★　★　★

The morning of the new day was spent in crossing unbroken ground, terrain which was taxing to both horses and riders. It seemed devoid of water holes and streams, and the water canteens were frequently in use by midday.

Perry kept coughing on dust and Cal became drowsy. The latter made an effort to keep awake, but he could not refrain from grumbling on occasion.

'Say, Simon,' he queried, 'are we ridin' faster today, or is the sun hotter? Or are we jest gettin' tired?'

'A little of all three, I'd say, amigo. Ridin' between trails always gets arduous after an hour or two. Maybe if we give ourselves somethin' to aim at, it'll make us feel better.'

Cal scanned the skyline ahead of them. 'How far would you say that ridge is from here?'

The ridge in question was a long smooth hogsback running east and west. The federal marshal studied it for a long time before giving his answer. 'It's a good place to aim for. I'd say nearly three hours' ride. If nothin' develops by the time we get there, we'll consider makin' early camp somewhere near it. What do you say to that?'

'It suits me fine,' Cal replied.

Counting an hour off for rest, the journey to the northern side of the ridge took just over four hours. No incidents of any kind had occurred. When they reined in just short of the talus at the foot of the ridge, a lazy bird of prey sailed through the sky high above them, and a jackrabbit scampered from one grassy clump to another ten yards away.

By tacit consent they dismounted, took a smoke and loosened and rocked their saddles. There was still no water available, and the horses had to make do with yellowing grass.

'It's a long way round the ridge, if we go further,' Cal observed.

'This side is not very comfortable for travellers, amigo, an' there's a path runs up the side of the ridge. How about pushin' up an' over an' trustin' to a change of luck.'

Cal watched the eagle for another minute or so and then nodded. He was the first to tighten his saddle and put his mount at the gradient. Perry followed him. They rode for about a furlong and then dismounted to give the horses a better chance of conserving their stamina.

Around eight hundred feet from the starting point they topped the gently rounded crest of the ridge and looked at the vista on the south side. Perhaps two miles further south a big, winding creek threaded its placid way through fairly lush vegetation. The sight of it brightened the faces of the two tired and thirsty riders. When the descent was completed, they rested the horses again. There was no difficulty in getting them to do the last lap. The animals had smelled the water.

About six hundred yards separated them from the water when a rifle shot sounded south of the creek. Both riders reined in.

'Huntin', I suppose,' Perry remarked thoughtfully.

'This calls for caution, though,' Cal emphasized.

When the distance had been halved they dismounted and walked at their horses' heads, hoping that they would not give away their presence to the hunter or hunters. Every man out in the open was possibly a Forester to them, until he had been proved otherwise.

The last fifty yards was rather a trial of nerves. Somewhere upstream they could hear the faint crackle of firewood burning, and an occasional call suggested that more than one man was relaxing by the fire.

Thick foliage and trees of the willow type hid them as they consulted quite close to the bank.

'Those could well be the boys we're lookin' for,' Cal whispered.

'I know it,' Perry returned. 'So let's water the horses an' then move closer, on this side.'

It was hard work keeping the horses

from striding into the creek, but they succeeded in doing so with a continuous effort. Soon they had finished refreshing themselves and were cautiously moving upstream around a loop in the creek.

At a distance of something over two hundred yards they caught their first glimpse of the smoke from the camp fire. Perry at once pulled out his glass and focused on the fire.

'The Forester boys are sittin' around the fire finishin' a meal. It looks to me as if another of their number, the little half-breed you mentioned, is actually in the creek takin' a swim.'

'We could take a few shots at them from here, but it wouldn't do any good,' Cal observed. 'Too much screenin' foliage in the way. Besides, we'd lose the surprise element an' give them a chance to pull out.'

'So let's go nearer, an' tackle them from two different angles on this side,' the marshal suggested.

And that was what they did. They

detoured away from the bank, rode forward as far as seemed possible without giving away their position, and then dismounted, walking the horses still nearer. In a small hollow, about seventy yards from the water, they pegged the animals and catfooted forward with their weapons.

Cal took the more direct route, and Marshal Perry moved about another fifty yards further east, so as to menace the camp from the wider angle.

As soon as Cal was in position among the screening foliage, he started to look around him. To the rear, the terrain was flat except for a small mound and an occasional clump of gnarled scrub oak. Across the water, he could see the heads and shoulders of the Foresters as they lolled about and smoked. There was a small inlet on the far side and a slim peninsula of earth was high enough to screen the resting outlaws. Of Juan Torres there was no sign, but judging by the occasional shout from the fire he was somewhere in the water.

Perry opened up with the first shot, deliberately hitting the cooking pot hanging above the fire and causing Red Forester to duck away from the ricochet.

'Hold it right there, you Foresters! You have guns trained on you from two angles!'

Red was already out of sight from Cal's angle, after ducking, and Morgan's head also disappeared before the peace officer had fully delivered his challenge and warning. Perry pumped shells into the vicinity of the fire, sending burning twigs flying and blasting away small stones.

Morgan gave one roar of anger and then the other bank was quiet.

Suddenly, Perry yelled: 'Look out, Cal! The swimmer!'

Cal, who had just fired two shots at the camp, put up the barrel of his weapon and saw the flat black hat of the swarthy man as he swam hard for the reeds downstream of the inlet. Without pause, Cal lined up his Winchester and took aim. He was about to fire at the weaving head when he remembered how he had felt when under fire in water near the Gallon place.

He hesitated for mere seconds, and in that time the swimmer plunged beneath the surface and disappeared into the reeds. Before Cal had time to blame himself a powerful ominous boom sounded behind him, coming from the direction of the wooded mound.

Upstream, Simon Perry gave a cry of alarm. Without being told, he knew that this latest weapon was the dreaded Sharps carbine, the one used with such deadly effect by Forest Jack. He felt certain at that moment that Jack was the marksman, and that he was shadowing the other men as a sort of guard and outrider. A second shot severed a small limb of the tree under which he was sheltering and dropped it across his shoulders.

Cal wanted to shout and tell that he

knew of the development, but for nearly a minute he was at a loss for words. Sounds on the opposite bank seemed to suggest that the Forester brothers were about to ride off. Perhaps that was a good thing for the two men who had thought to get the better of them.

While Cal was thinking, the flat black hat drifted down the creek near the far bank. He was not fool enough to think that its owner was dead. The hat could have been lifted when the swimmer ducked under water.

Abruptly, a course of action presented itself to Cal. He yelled: 'Into the water, Simon! Get down the bank an' be prepared to cross at short notice! You hear me?'

Perry called back in the affirmative. A third missile from the Sharps passed within a foot of his head. Cal turned and plunged into the long grass, worming his way with all speed towards the hollow where the horses were pegged out.

As he moved forward a probing shot

sought his hideout, striking the foliage within a yard of where he had been. He kept going, while Perry fired back at the mound and then slipped into the creek, wondering if anyone on the far bank was witnessing his entry.

The next minute or two dragged. For once the marksman had missed the movement of the crawling man. He was also a little puzzled by the lack of return fire, and the quietness across the creek. Cal achieved his object, the hollow. He plunged down into the bottom of it, tightened the saddles, mounted up on his own beast and prepared to race the two horses over the seventy yards to the creek.

He knew that he was taking a deadly risk, but it still seemed to be the best thing to do. Without the horses they might never get mounted again, and on foot their plight could become desperate so far away from towns.

Both animals responded well. Cal gave the sorrel more of the rowel than ever before. He topped the rise at the rim of the hollow and rode forward with his back bent close over the beast's neck. The black responded nobly; at times it pulled away and then came close again. This all out effort, coupled with a fusillade from Perry, aimed at the mound, enabled the auburn-headed rider to accomplish most of the distance without dodging shells.

It was in the last fifteen yards that the Sharps opened up again and the muscles of his back began to twitch. The first missile passed closely over his right shoulder. A second nicked the saddle on the stallion's back. The third, more carefully sighted than the rest, came late.

Cal had glimpsed a patch of hanging willow fronds with no trunk underneath them. Yipping loudly, he drove both horses over the bank. Side by side they plunged into the creek, controlled by the one man. It was while they were actually going through the air in the jump that the third shot ripped through the air towards them.

The rider knew a moment of intense relief as it whined over his head once again. The three bodies hit the water with an almighty splash. Before they had fully recovered their breath, Perry had launched himself out from the bank with his shoulder weapon held high. Cal turned the horses and helped his partner into the saddle.

One nod was sufficient to send the horses swimming across the creek towards the inlet where the outlaw had bathed. Foliage on the shore they had left screened them for most of the way across, but they could not be sure that the swimmer was not waiting for them or that the man with the Sharps was not hurrying down to the water's edge.

Actually, Forest Jack had miscalculated. He set off later than he need have done for the water's edge, and in so doing he missed his chance of firing on the two mounted men as they emerged on the south side.

No bullets came at them from the southern bank. Nor did the Sharps man attempt to follow them across. For over an hour they waited for him to show himself, but all remained still. He had apparently melted into the landscape.

That night they camped some distance away, and they did without the comfort of a fire.

13

After their harrowing experience at the creek, the partners were not anxious to clash with their opponents so far away from towns and help. They moved south for a few miles and then turned east, following out Perry's belief that there was some connection between the Foresters and the Circle S.

Two more nights were spent in the open. On one of those nights, a distant camp fire suggested that the outlaws were still heading for Circle S property. Another far off glimpse of grouped riders in daytime appeared to confirm this theory.

On the third day after the last clash, the partners decided to take a chance on their theory and go ahead of the outlaws. This way they might achieve a surprise of sorts with help close at hand. It was fortunate that Cal had known the area since childhood. His knowledge kept them out of any difficulties due to the local geography.

By three o'clock in the afternoon they were on high ground looking down on the wire fence which marked the limit of the Circle S's rolling acres. Perry smiled indulgently, thinking that Cal was the heir to all this land, and that he was still a very modest young man. He pointed forward.

'That line cabin stands out like a sore thumb, amigo. Do you think your unwanted visitors will be brash enough to use it?'

Cal thought about the question, all the time rubbing his chin. 'I don't see why not. This is the north-west boundary of our range. We have no beeves up this way this year, an' no one ever comes near it. There'd be no reason for the regular 'punchers to come this way. It's too isolated.'

'So they could use it, in passin'. Well, I for one wouldn't specially want to tangle with the renegades right there.

Not unless we had some kind of distinct advantage. And I don't suppose a line cabin could provide that.'

'It's a more elaborate buildin' than most line cabins,' Cal explained. 'There's only the one room, of course, but it has a cellar. Two men built it some years ago. One of them was a nervous type an' he insisted on buildin' the cellar in case they were attacked this far from the ranch by rustlers.'

'Let's go down there an' look at it.'

The marshal sounded enthusiastic, but Cal used his spyglass on the surrounding countryside before he consented to go forward. It was no use planning any sort of a surprise if they were already observed. When they had crossed the wire and reached the building, the horses were left around the back, out of sight from anyone approaching from the north or the west.

Perry stepped inside and sniffed around. There was a stove in the middle, a table, shelves, and a few chairs. The men who had been isolated in this north-western outpost of the spread had put down a thin plank floor for extra comfort. The cellar which Cal had mentioned was like a trapdoor in the centre, located underneath the table.

Perry fingered his chin while he looked down at it. 'If outlaws come here they won't arrive until the daylight has almost gone. Maybe they won't notice the trap at once. All we want is a few minutes in which to have them all assembled together, then we can jump them.'

Cal pulled aside the table and lifted up the door in the floor. It was roomy enough for two men, and the builders had provided two small crude air shafts so that suffocation was out of the question. The partners were very thoughtful as they crawled out.

Cal remarked: 'We'd have to get in there in good time. It wouldn't do to be caught in the cellar by that shocker from the lumber camp.'

'At the best it would be a gamble, an'

we'd have to stache the horses away at a good distance.'

'But they won't expect us to be up ahead of them,' Cal argued, 'an' I know a place where they'll never find cayuses. Don't forget, this is part of my home territory.'

'All right, then, we'll try it,' Perry suggested soberly.

Cal's hiding place for the horses was a hollow some two hundred and fifty yards away with a concealing fringe of scrub and grass. It was an obvious place to leave animals, because there was plenty of grass in the bottom. Within half an hour they had prepared a meal over a fire in the hollow. If secrecy was to be ensured, it would not do to light the stove in the cabin.

One hour later, they backtracked with a great show of caution and smoked for a while, concealed from the land beyond the boundary by the rear wall. For several minutes, they discussed the various things which had happened to them since they teamed up together. To Cal it seemed very much longer than just a few days since he made the acquaintance of his riding partner.

Neither of them doubted that the Foresters would come, nor that they would avail themselves of the seemingly empty line cabin.

Presently, their restlessness made them go inside the building with their weapons. It was too early to go below; for a while they lolled about, wanting to smoke and not daring to in case the smell of tobacco gave away their presence. Then they dozed, taking turns of half an hour apiece.

Towards six o'clock, Cal was on watch. 'I see them, Simon. Up on that slope, where we first sighted the cabin. They're early.'

'Land's sakes, so they really are here. We must watch until they start down this way an' then hide ourselves. While we've been keeping watch through that front window, I hope we haven't been visible to anyone else through the other pane at the rear.'

'Too late for doubts now, pardner.'

Ten minutes later, the Foresters and Torres started down the slope. They were maintaining vigilance, but not excessively so. Obviously they believed the shack to be empty. Two or three minutes of careful effort were necessary before the two big men were down in the dark pit of the cellar. Above them they had manoeuvred the trapdoor into place and contrived to have the table partially covering it.

'It's a good job that sun is well over towards the west. We couldn't do with its rays focused on the door of this dugout,' Cal murmured.

'Anythin' botherin' you, Cal? You looked troubled the last time you spied out of the window.'

'The third man. It must be the Mexican. He's wearin' a hat jest like mine. It seems different seein' as how he had that flat black hat the other times when we saw him. He lost that at the creek back there.'

'Are you thinkin' it might be your brother's hat, Cal?' Perry asked gently.

'If it is I hope the present wearer has as little luck in it as Bob did!'

For once the auburn-haired young man sounded thoroughly ruthless.

★ ★ ★

The trio of outlaws jogged gently up to the front of the cabin and swung out of leather. Juan Torres seemed by far the most nervous of them. Seeing his agitation, Red Forester sniffed while his brother murmured: 'No cattle in sight, an' no signs of life. Quit worryin', Juan. An' remember Jack is about some place. We won't take any harm.'

Morgan led the way into the cabin and sniffed the dust. 'Come on in, boys, make yourselves at home. An' remember we have a buddy works for the Circle S, so we ain't exactly ordinary intruders.'

Red managed a chuckle and the small half-breed's face relaxed. In they went, taking their weapons with them. Even as they did so, Forest Jack, the unknown quantity in the cross country chase, rode out of timber onto the high ground where both groups of arrivals had first sighted the cabin. Jack had come from a route rather more to the north, and for that reason he was not aware that two groups had recently covered that same ground.

He sat his buckskin between two stunted trees and peered down at the shack, wondering if his kin were missing him. Merely as an exercise, he dismounted, pulled out his Sharps and stood with it to his shoulder, pointing it at the moving men seen through the front window. Having assured himself that he could fire on anyone down there, should the opportunity arise, he put up his weapon and hunkered down, working on the makings of a cigarette. He was calm enough at the time, and if anyone had hinted that he would not complete the rolling of the smoke, he would have been greatly surprised.

In the cabin, Morgan said: 'Well, Juan, are you satisfied now? If so, how about leavin' us for a few minutes while you collect wood for the stove?'

Perry nudged Cal, in the dark, down below. Now was the time to show themselves, otherwise one of the trio would be missing. Better get them all at once, if possible. A concerted heave of the shoulders sent up the trapdoor and the table which was resting on it. The two men from under the trap appeared like jack-in-the-boxes, bouncing up and pointing their guns in opposite directions.

Red and Torres were at the front of the room, Torres slightly nearer the door. Morgan was at the rear. In fact he had been peering out of the window there. All three sprang about as the furniture crashed and their enemies appeared. For once, the sight of pointing guns prevented them from a lightning draw.

'Hold it, all of you! We know exactly who you are an' it'll be jest as effective if we take you dead as alive!'

Perry talked with the voice of authority. Without undue haste, all three began to raise their hands. The marshal was watching closely as Torres glanced towards Red. Perry's eyes followed the glance, and in a split second, Torres' hands had dipped to his waist. Up came his right hand gun, beating Perry to the trigger by a split second.

Two guns roared in the enclosed space, buffering ears and playing on taut nerves. Torres' bullet made a shallow groove on the outer side of the federal man's left upper arm, just below the tip of the shoulder bone. Perry's bullet missed its target, holing the glass of the front window. Perceiving the danger, Cal took his eyes and gun off Morgan and fired a hastily aimed snapshot at Torres.

Cal's bullet missed and Torres was in the act of firing back when the unexpected happened. The distant boom of the Sharps did not carry to them, but the bullet aimed from it hit Torres in the back and knocked him to the ground at the crucial moment.

Perry, who had crouched low, after being hit, straightened up and threatened the broken-nosed man again, just as he had his hands on his gun butts. Morgan, who had hesitated, found himself looking down the muzzle of Cal's smoking Colt once again.

'Now, let's all take it easy,' Cal ordered calmly.

Morgan cursed briefly and Red spat towards the window. For the moment, the Foresters were under control. Perhaps their half brother's mistake had for a time taken the confidence out of them.

'A pity your buddy was wearin' another man's hat,' Cal went on. 'Jack wouldn't have killed him, otherwise. It's good to know Jack makes mistakes, too.'

Cal threw aside his own hat and vaulted lightly out of the cellar. He took Morgan's guns and then moved around to disarm Red.

'Well done, Cal,' Perry remarked calmly. 'Jest don't go too close to that window, in case our marksman has another go.'

Cal grinned. For the time, he was well in control.

14

As long as Forest Jack was up there on the slope with his Sharps, he was a menace. Cal and his partner were thinking hard before they attempted to leave the building. Red and Morgan were secured at the wrists by their gun belts. They waited in a corner, glowering and watching, while the other two talked in whispers well away from them.

Presently, Perry hefted both hand guns and Cal turned his attention to the crumpled figure of Torres. Forest Jack, they had figured, had to learn that he had shot one of his own kind in mistake. His confidence had to be undermined, and the knowledge of such an accident ought to do the trick.

It was difficult to pick up Torres by the shoulders and hoist him forward towards the door, but Cal managed the job. He then levered the door open with his foot and straightened Torres in the entrance. Forest Jack then had a clear view of him. Cal had reasoned that Jack would not fire until he had had a close look. He would expect his partners to emerge in full control.

For a few seconds, Cal held the corpse of Torres poised there, and then he pushed the body forward, standing smartly aside in cover as it crumpled to the ground and the hat fell off. The Sharps did not boom again. The lack of action seemed to confirm that Jack had the body in view and had recognized it.

With extra guns in their pockets and stuffed in their belts, the two men in control then planned to emerge. Perry's groove was losing a trickle of blood, but he insisted that he was not in need of immediate attention. Cal led the with-drawal, using the bulky body of Morgan as his shield from any shooting on the hill slope. At the hitch rail, he ordered the outlaw to mount up. Keeping Morgan and his horse between himself and the marksman, he untied Torres' pinto and controlled the move to the rear.

As soon as the cabin was between them and the position of Forest Jack, Cal mounted the pinto and waited for the arrival of Perry. The marshal achieved the same move with as little difficulty. For sure, Jack had seen his earlier mistake. He would be a little more cautious from this time forward.

The waiting sorrel and black were soon cinched up for the ride and the quartette set off across Circle S range with an hour or two of daylight in hand.

A little after nine p.m., Chang, the Simpsons' diminutive Chinese cook, spotted the arrival of the four men on horseback from north range. He scurried away to inform others, and by the time the quartette were approaching the cluster of buildings, upwards of ten cowhands and the rest of the family had foregathered to meet them.

Cal took control. 'Howdy, folks. It sure is good to see you all again. I'm goin' to have to ask you to keep right away from these two hombres, though, because they're the Forester brothers, wanted outlaws an' my pardner an' me, we can't rightly relax until we've delivered them to the nearest lock-up.'

Henry Simpson limped closer, patted his son's leg and appeared to be pleased to see him. His brow furrowed as he looked over the prisoners, and he wanted to ask questions about how they had been captured, but Bob was buried now and Calvin seemed to have adopted his mantle of authority.

'Where's Raybold, Pa?'

'Here I am, an' who's askin' for me?'

The segundo appeared quite suddenly from the furthest stable building and looked surprised when he saw the four grouped horses. Cal explained who the prisoners were and drew Raybold aside.

'Now see here, Larry, there's another man at large, a relation of these boys. So I want to know that you'll be keepin' a sharp lookout for strangers around the buildings. If you think anyone is prowlin' around, investigate. You hear me?'

Raybold nodded. 'Are you goin' into town with these boys?'

'Sure. Along with Marshal Perry, there. The Foresters will want some watchin', too. Let's hope the town jail is strong enough.'

Raybold went away then to clean himself up. Two of the regular hands kept a watch on the prisoners while Cal and Perry, one at a time, slipped away to freshen up and take on some coffee. Ten minutes later, they were ready to ride again.

Mollie, Cal's sister, ran after them and overtook them as they reached the gate. Cal frowned, but he drew aside long enough to exchange a few words with her.

'What's troublin' you, Mollie?'

'A whole lot, if I could get a few answers, Cal. Why do these sort of men come ridin' to the Circle S? What have we done to attract them? Can you answer me that?'

'Sis, there is a connection with Bob's death, I think. I can't tell you all the answers now, but we shall know them fairly soon. You made a good job of dressin' Simon's arm. He'll be pleased about that. See you soon, Mollie. *Adios*.'

The girl stood aside, looking troubled. Cal sent the sorrel through the gate and went after the other three. He left Mollie to close up after him.

★ ★ ★

In Wildcat there had been a few changes since Cal rode out of town. The town marshal, for instance, had finished his term of office and been replaced by Chad Martin, the bluff hearty fight promoter who had insisted on Cal going into the ring with Sailor McCardoe.

Martin greeted Cal quite warmly as the latter hitched his gelding to the rail outside the office. Cal shook his hand and returned the scrutiny. The new star toter had grown a short beard and moustache. The beard was close-trimmed and the moustache had been waxed. He was an imposing figure in a black outfit, but Cal knew that he was inexperienced in his new type of work.

'Who are your friends, Cal?'

'Federal Marshal Simon Perry an' a couple of badly wanted outlaws. The Forester brothers.'

Martin cut short his greeting to the federal officer and stared hard at the outlaws. Some six or eight other men were gathering round and also showing a lot of curiosity.

'Let's get these boys inside before we attract too much attention, Chad,' Cal suggested. 'They're dynamite an' they'll have to spend the night in your lock-up.'

Martin whistled, but he stood back and allowed the other two to escort the prisoners indoors. The only other man in the office was old Charlie Parnes, the official jailer. Charlie was not far off seventy years in age. Time had rendered his tall figure thin and stooping. In fact, he was only an odd job man for the marshal. No one actually regarded him any more as a force to be reckoned with.

Chad Martin took the keys from a hook and led the way into the corridor at the rear of the office, which ran along the front of the one large bar-fronted cell. He opened the door and stood well back while Red Forester paced in, followed by his brother.

Side by side, the outlaws sat on the long wooden bench which served as a bunk for one man. Morgan said: 'Make with the food, lawman.' He spoke softly, but there was still an edge of menace in his voice.

Martin locked the door after them and came away. In the main office, he talked some more with his visitors.

'Maybe you an' I ought to stay the night in town, Simon,' Cal suggested. 'Jest in case there's an attempt to free these two.'

'I figure that would be the safest

thing to do,' the federal man returned.

He seemed quite calm, but his upper arm was troubling him a little. Martin and Parnes heard the discussion and began to look apprehensive.

'You think there ought to be a man in the office all night, Mr Perry?' Martin queried.

'I think that might be best. You could leave your jailer, if you like. Cal an' me, we'll stay within hailin' distance. So you don't need to stick around yourself.'

Martin looked happier for this advice. He was rubbing his chin rather shrewdly when Cal shot him a glance of interrogation.

'Well, Chad, as the new marshal, what are you thinkin'?'

The ex-boxing promoter nodded and started to pace the scarred wooden floor. 'First off, I think you two boys must have had yourselves quite a time before you apprehended these outlaws. Secondly, judgin' by the way you talked and looked when we discussed keepin' guard tonight, I'd say you were possibly rather keen to have somebody try an' spring these two. Am I right?'

Cal chuckled, but Perry supplied the information. 'The missin' man is a bigger menace than these two put together. If he happened along to get them out, it might give us a chance to round him up without spending half our lives searching the county for him.'

'And his name is?'

'Forest Jack, or Jack Forest, or probably Jack Forester,' Cal explained quietly. 'Besides this fellow, we think there's another contact of the gang in this area, so if you come along an' see either one of us actin' kind of strange towards a man you know well, don't be surprised, eh?'

Martin promised to keep calm in all circumstances. He sent Charlie Parnes to the nearest eating house to fetch food for the prisoners and entertained his tired guests for a half hour while the old jailer came back.

At that juncture, Cal and Simon left together. Outside, a man in a brown derby had the gumption to come along and ask the question which was on everybody's lips.

'Say, gents, those two prisoners in there. Is it true they're the notorious Forester brothers?'

Cal glanced at his partner, who answered. 'Yes, they are. But we don't want too much publicity tonight in case there's an attempt to break them out of jail again.'

The questioner thanked them and said that he fully understood. He moved off through the small jostling crowd and took some of them with him to the nearest saloon.

'I'll watch first,' Cal offered. 'You get some rest an' prop up that arm. If I need to be relieved I'll send old Charlie along to the hotel to get you. Leave a note of your room on the reception desk.'

Perry squeezed Cal's shoulder and at once agreed. He moved off up the street, leaving the horses behind. Cal took them along to the nearest livery, then hurriedly purchased a light meal and took it with him to a vacant office on the first floor of a building right opposite the peace office.

Later, Marshal Martin took him some coffee before leaving his office in the charge of the old man.

15

The sky was not really black in the region of the Circle S until after eleven o'clock. By that time, the sky was like black velvet and almost everyone was asleep. Even the cows, a furlong away on home range, were particularly still. In both stables only one horse showed any signs of fidgeting. None of its quadruped companions were disturbed.

The tune which was played on the muted harp was not really a tune at all. Before the melody was completed the sound died, and anyone who was a light sleeper could well have been forgiven if they thought they had dreamed up the sound.

Mollie Simpson was one of those who found it hard to sleep. Her mother had gone off without any difficulty and her father, Henry, slept soundly, although he had been wide wake for an hour after his head touched the pillow.

Mollie, a girl of deep sensitivity, kept going over and over in her mind about Cal and his recent affairs. Of late, she fully realized the anguish he must have suffered when he returned to the ranch without his brother and more or less shouldered the blame for having failed him at the time when he was most needed.

Since that time when Cal had ridden away, life had dragged. She had lived with the idea that he, also, might never come back. And now he was back again, looking rather tired and drawn, but working incessantly and with a splendid new air of authority which augured well for the ranch, if he ever settled down. Moreover, he had faced sudden death on more than one occasion, and, judging by his attitude and that of his magnificent federal marshal friend, more danger still lay ahead.

After mulling all this over in her mind for an hour, Mollie gave up the idea of sleeping in her bed. She got out and rapidly dressed herself in a pair of denim levis, a white shirt and a woollen riding jacket. Cramming a flat-topped hat over her bell of copper-coloured hair she tiptoed out of the house, took a quick look around from the gallery, and then ran lightly across to the galley.

Chang always left plenty of fuel in his stove and there was never anyone there at night. She let herself in, smelling the homely tang of the burning wood, and crossed to the bench which was angled across the front of the range and topped by a padded cushion.

She pulled on a glove and cautiously opened the front of the range so that the red embers showed and the room was given a pleasing glow. Sighing rather heavily, she stretched herself out on the bench, put her hat under her head and simply stared into the fire.

Mollie had heard the few brief notes on the mouth harp, but she had thought nothing of it. The outside world was full of sounds of one sort and another; some man-made, others animal-made. Besides, she had not been back from school long, and all sounds about the ranch were relatively new to her. She had never been allowed to be fearful of night sounds.

The musical sounds were as good as forgotten when the next set of noises came to her ears. She had been in the galley for perhaps twenty minutes when a board creaked back in the house. She sensed rather than heard the front door open, and raised her brows in the dark as someone in soft footgear left the main building and came stealthily over the same route as she had taken.

Who could it be? Had someone heard her leave and come after her to see what she was doing? Or was it someone with a more sinister motive? Larry Raybold, the segundo, had been very thoughtful since Cal talked to him earlier in the evening. Just then she did not want to meet anyone from the house, other than her mother and father, and quite certainly the stealthy footsteps did not belong to either of them.

Raybold had occupied a room in the house for over a week now. Henry had to depend upon him more than before: now that Bob was dead and Cal away from home. She was thinking about Raybold, and yet in no way certain that the feet were his, as the footsteps approached.

The girl's heart was thumping harder than she had ever known it when the person unseen paused at the door and then went on past. He rounded the end of the building and catfooted to the north-eastern corner. There, to her surprise, he stopped. She heard the sounds of a subdued greeting.

The knowledge that another man was there in the darkness — had probably been there unknown for some time — made her clutch her throat in panic. And yet at this juncture, she did not know the nature of her fear. Why was she panicking? Was it simply that she was facing certain unknown things at a time when everyone else should be asleep?

Her breath came and went with difficulty because she was attempting to make it quieter than usual. There was a window within four or five feet of the whispering men. She thought they might see her through it if they took the trouble just to move a few feet. But they talked on, showing no signs of moving.

'It was good to hear the sounds of that mouth harp again, Jack. Even though recent happenings have rather shaken me. How did the boys get jumped by young Simpson an' that federal marshal?'

'That's a good question, Larry. Especially as I'd been followin' them at a distance. They moved in on that big line cabin up the north-west of Circle S range. They couldn't have known it had a hidin' place in it — '

'A cellar,' Raybold put in hoarsely. 'These two jaspers hid in the cellar an' jumped them when they came in.'

'They did so, sure enough. An' I

made it worse. I gave the hat I took from the dead son, Bob Simpson, to Juan Torres, an' when the shootin' started in the shack I saw this figure in the undented hat. I had to blast off quickly, because I knew the boys were up against it. I hit the man in the tall hat, all right, thinkin' it was this other hombre, the younger Simpson. Only I made a mistake an' salivated Torres instead. That must have shaken Morgan and Red, because the other two took control again an' I wasn't able to help. They used my brothers for shields, as they came out.'

'Yer, that sure is bad for the boys, Jack,' Raybold commiserated. 'When did you figure this young galoot with the auburn hair was another Simpson?'

'Only a short while ago. I knew he must have some sort of a connection with what's been goin' on, but it was not until I was ridin' across this range that I twigged it. But that's enough of idle talk, Larry. This night we've got to act to set the boys free. Every hour we delay, the more likely it is they'll head back for the pen — or worse!'

By this time, Mollie had heard enough to know that she was hearing a conversation between Raybold and some old outlaw friend, probably one who had a lot to do with her brother's present worries. Moreover, if she had heard rightly, the man with the mouth harp was probably Bob's killer.

In order not to scream, she pushed the brim of her hat between her teeth and at the same time blocked her ears. She felt she could not hear any more of this secret talk without accidentally revealing her presence.

Some five minutes later, she uncovered her ears to know if they had gone. They were still there and talking quite animatedly. Raybold was explaining to his audience of one how he had bribed Slim Tillot to draw Cal away from Bob at the crucial time to make the ambush and robbery easy.

The other man applauded his planning and in his turn said how easy it had been to knock Bob Simpson out of his saddle with the Sharps. This was all Mollie could take. She slipped to the ground and cowered in front of the range with her head in her hands until long after the conspirators had left.

★ ★ ★

A distant chiming clock had struck midnight and actually roused Cal who had dozed when he first had the sensation that all was not so quiet in the town. The peace office showed no more life than when Charlie Parnes had turned down the lamp over the desk an hour earlier.

A full five minutes elapsed before any distinct sound confirmed the young man's earlier suspicions. His brows went up in surprise when he heard a horse being walked along Main from the eastern end of town. If this was a wayfarer he had picked a particularly unusual and relatively unpopular time for drifting into town. One thing became clearer as the horse and rider cut down on the distance to the peace office; it was most certainly not Forest Jack.

Nevertheless, remembering the unknown contact in the local area, Cal reached for his weapons. He knelt under the window of the vacant office and peered down the street, wishing he had night vision as good as that of the remarkable old man who had so nearly shot him on more than one occasion.

Soon the figure hunched in the saddle assumed a definite shape. Cal peered down at the newcomer with his hat brim flattened by the window pane. He kept quite still, and easily remained unnoticed, but his surprise was great when the horse was angled to the hitch rail outside of the peace office, and none other than Larry Raybold casually slid to the ground, as though this was any ordinary hour of daytime.

Cal recollected his last brief interview with Raybold. He had especially asked him to be alert around the ranch in case there was trouble that night; and now, here was the segundo, rolling into town and boldly arriving at the peace office. Certainly this was not a good time to visit, considering what might happen if Forest Jack came along in an equally bold fashion.

★ ★ ★

Unknown to Cal, the cell part of the big office had already been approached from the rear. The man he feared most had already arrived. He was carefully hidden outside the window with the bars on it, studying the local geography and wondering if he would have to do anything really drastic to ensure that his half brothers got out in one piece.

As he paced up and down silently in mocassined feet, Forest Jack tried to work out all the possibilities. He had already found two useful ponies hitched to a rail in the next street. They had been overlooked by two cow-punchers spending their month's pay on local booze.

He felt that if he had to he could lead the two prisoners across the backs without any difficulty. Weapons they could take from the office, given a minute or two in which to operate. Failing that, they would have to make a strike elsewhere, on the way out of town.

Jack thought hard about Larry. He was no Forester, but he had been loyal in the past. It was a pity he was not in a hurry to be active as a law-breaker at the moment, but he could still be of use to them. Of course, if anything went wrong and the forces of law and order tied him in with the regular gang he would be only too glad to get clear of town and ride the owlhoot trail as of old, with the others.

But Larry, not being a Forester by blood, and not having done anything particularly bad against the law for a whole long time might want watching. He might have lost his touch for when it came to thwarting the law. Therefore, Jack was prepared to act entirely on his own. That way, his brothers were doubly safeguarded.

Having ascertained the distance up to the barred opening in the wall, Jack took down from his saddle horn the lariat which had not been used by him much of late. He moved in close to the wall, hoisted the end of it up to the opening and looped it round a single well-fitted bar. Having done that he pulled down on the strip of rawhide to make it as inconspicuous as possible and twanged a single quiet note upon his mouth harp.

There was no answering sound from within the cell, but after another minute someone stirred and a boot apparently knocked the wall as the sleeper turned over.

Jack pocketed the mouth harp and retired to stand beside his sinewy buckskin. When he wanted, he could stand as still as a statue, quelling all emotion. This was one of those occasions.

16

Raybold noticed that there was no other horse hitched within a short distance, as he pulled up at the peace office and quietly slid to the ground. His mount, a skewbald, pawed the earth as though asking to have the saddle girth slackened. It asked in vain.

Its master stood beside it for several seconds, exploring his lantern jaw and the crescent of scar near his left eye. He had been out of touch with gunplay and robberies since the Foresters went to the pen and he stayed in the clear.

Of late, he had admitted to himself his fancy for young Miss Mollie, the daughter of his employers. If anything happened to Cal Mollie would be the one to inherit. She would have no one to share the spread with, and if she were married then her husband would be a rich man in his own right. He felt that he could be that husband if he were not embarrassed from outside.

It was a pity, in a way, that the Foresters had been sprung when they were, and that they had galloped towards Wildcat and the Circle S instead of killing and stealing in some other part of the territory. But the Foresters were hard men to cross. This far he had not had a chance to speak with the brothers alone. Maybe they still resented the fact that they had done time, whereas he had remained free with a clean record.

Forest Jack had made it quite clear that they had to be sprung, and that very night; which was the reason he had ridden into town when he could have been sleeping soundly in his bed in the Simpson ranch house.

For perhaps two minutes he remained standing by the impatient skewbald. He was thinking that he would like to know the exact whereabouts of the federal marshal and of

Cal Simpson, who had returned with the Foresters to town. This pair had behaved with a show of great caution out at the ranch. Surely, they wouldn't abandon the outlaws to the makeshift forces of law and order in Wildcat?

Raybold was reluctant to enter the office. The skewbald, however, swung its neck round and tucked him under the chin with its muzzle. He knew he ought to be moving, and he walked across to the door, gently trying the handle.

It turned easily and the door moved inwards. He pushed it further and stepped indoors, closing the door and putting his back against it. Charlie Parnes was the only person on duty, and he was asleep with his head across his folded arm which rested on the marshal's desk.

Old Parnes' stomach rumbled. The swivel chair shifted a little under him, and the note on which he was snoring altered. He appeared to be going on sleeping, however, and Raybold slowly moved on stealthy feet nearer to the desk.

He was licking his lips and hefting out his Colt when a sudden noise startled him and made him withdraw a step. A steady thumping was coming from the street. Instead of pistol-whipping the sleeping jailer he tiptoed across to the window and peered out. He mouthed a mute curse as he saw that the skewbald was impatiently kicking the boards of the sidewalk with one of its fore shoes.

'Eh? Oh, sorry, amigo, I didn't know we had visitors!'

Charlie Parnes was awake now, even if his faculties were not very sharp. This put the whole explosive situation in a different light. Raybold took a grip on himself, forced a grin and crossed to the desk, where Parnes was knuckling his bloodshot eyes and looking rather surprised.

'Did I disturb you, Charlie?'

'Can't rightly say if you did or not, but somethin' did otherwise I'd be asleep right now, Larry.' He scratched his head as though he did not fully comprehend the circumstances. 'Can't rightly understand why you ain't asleep yourself, at such an hour as this. Something important must have brought you out here. Would you like to tell me about it?'

'Should I talk to the marshal?'

Parnes started to gesture and splutter. Raybold grinned and waved him back to silence. 'All right, I know the kind of fellow Martin is. Sure, I'll talk to you. It's like this. Those two hombres you have back there, the Foresters, they were apprehended on Circle S soil. I expect you know that much?'

Parnes nodded hard. Mention of the Foresters had put his nerves on edge, so that he felt a lot less like talking to the Circle S segundo at this hour of the night.

'The fact is, Henry, my Boss, is a little concerned about them havin' ridden a long way, an' havin' turned up where they did. Henry asked me to come along and have a few words with them, with the permission of this office, of course, an' no chances to be taken.

'I'm sure you want to get back to sleep, Charlie, an' my Boss is an impatient man, so if you could see your way to put me through to the cell for a few minutes, I'll ask my questions an' clear out again, so's you'll be in peace. Now, what do you say?'

Raybold put on a beaming smile which emphasized his big jaw, and the uneven teeth in it. The smile grew narrower as he saw that Charlie would need more persuading. The old man was fidgeting and showing every sign of wanting to stay right away from the cell corridor, but Raybold did not think that he could sway the jailer to allow him to enter the rear of the building alone.

'Jest into the passage is all I ask, Charlie, an' make sure I'll be holden to you afterwards. It's a good thing for an elderly galoot to have important friends.'

Varying expressions flitted across the

lined face, but eventually Charlie looked bright for long enough to nod. This was all Raybold wanted to start him on his way. He picked up the big ring with the two keys on it and offered it to the jailer who took it.

The segundo gave Charlie plenty of time to gather himself together and to unlock the door to the passage. Charlie pulled open the door and cautiously looked through it. One of the Foresters, Red, was on the bench, and Morgan was stretched out on the floor. Both appeared to have been sleeping, but at that moment they opened an eye and took in the jailer.

To Raybold's surprise, Charlie pushed the key ring into his hand. The old man appeared to be fascinated by the two resting outlaws. He gestured for Raybold to return the keys to the office, but did not notice when the visitor retained them. Raybold pushed the ring up his arm and stepped a little closer to the bars, peering through them as though very curious about the actual appearance of the outlaws.

He said: 'You boys are Red and Morgan Forester? Is that right?'

Without any undue signs of excitement, the brothers moved into a sitting position. Morgan nodded, and Raybold responded with a slight show of excitement.

'That bein' so there are questions I have to ask you on behalf of my Boss, Henry Simpson. So listen good, boys, otherwise this will take a long time.'

Charlie Parnes was shifting his weight from one foot to the other, and finding it difficult not to bite his nails. A slight breeze came through from the main office. Charlie was the first to detect it.

'Hell an' tarnation, I'll be doggoned if that street door ain't blown open again!'

Seconds later, Cal Simpson appeared in the passage doorway. He nodded to Charlie who moved back again, further into the passage. Cal addressed himself to Raybold.

'Howdy, Larry, I guess I'm the last person you expected to step through this doorway. Well, I'm glad I made it in time. The fact is, you ought to be elsewhere, as you know. I'm practically certain why you came here an' I can guess what you intended to do. So I'm tellin' you real slowly to step well away from that door. Do you want me to spell it out for you?'

Tension built up in the small area. Red Morgan had risen to his feet and was standing by the outside wall of the cell. Morgan was on one knee, and considerably closer, no doubt hoping that he might get a chance to snatch the keys or a gun.

The next development, although it was expected by some, changed the mounting situation altogether.

Morgan was saying: 'What in tarnation is this young jasper talkin' about?'

'He's jumpin' to conclusions, I guess,

like he always used to do,' Raybold argued.

Charlie Parnes, oddly enough, was the first one to see the crack run down the back wall from the barred window. The wall was of adobe, and consequently a strong pull on it would cause it to fall. Cal knew something was happening, but for several seconds he did not know what.

Red moved his back in front of the crack, but it was only a matter of seconds later when the straining horse out at the back caused the bars, and the adobe around and beneath them, to rumble and fall outwards. Dust built up in front of the new hole.

Morgan coughed and groped his way further back. Raybold heaved Parnes in the direction of Cal, who was put off balance for a few seconds.

'I told you you were jumpin' to conclusions,' Raybold shouted hoarsely. 'That's the jasper you want to apprehend out there at the back! Now, act like your father's son! Make him proud of you!'

Cal ignored these meaningless words while Raybold sprang to the door, inserted the key and hurled himself into the cell.

'If we hurry we'll get this hombre out at the back!' Raybold added.

He acted as though he was on the level, elbowing Morgan to one side and Red to the other. He sprang for the hole in the wall, but not before Red had relieved him of a six-gun from his swinging holster. Red had weighed up the present situation and correctly interpreted Raybold's move as treachery. While Morgan picked himself up, alert and watching every small move, Raybold disappeared through the gap and was heard to scramble over the fallen debris on the outside.

Red lined up the gun on the jailer whose hand was trembling on the gun in his holster. The outlaw's mouth hardened, he fired and Parnes jerked back with a bullet in his shoulder. Cal shrugged away his surprise and drew his gun. He opened his mouth to shout a warning, but the deadly look in the eyes of the brothers told him this was not the time for it.

Ignoring the bars between them, he aimed at Red, squeezing his trigger as the other swung round on him. Cal fired twice. The first bullet nicked a shoulder and the second ripped into Red's chest, throwing him backwards against the rear wall with his knees buckling. Cal blinked as Red contrived to throw the gun across to Morgan.

The latter took it cleanly and turned to line it up on the one man who still barred their way to freedom. Cal saw the danger in the lethal frown on Morgan's face, and also in the gun's muzzle.

He steadied his gun hand and aimed for the chest of the second brother, wondering as he did so if Forest Jack was about to throw himself into the battle for survival. No gun appeared at the hole in the wall. Before anything could distract him, Cal fired two more shots. This time they were both on target. One hit Morgan just above the waistline, and the second hit flesh and bone below the neck.

As Morgan sank down to the floor, his eyes glazing, Cal coughed on gun smoke. He looked around him, expecting company at any time. None came. Instead of dashing into the demolished cell where the two wounded men were, he retreated through the office and made his way with caution around the back. Again, he found the area empty, and he spent two minutes exploring it for signs of the man who had pulled out the wall, and for Raybold.

Both men, and the horse which had done the pulling, had disappeared. Voices were sounding in the street now. Soon, men would be along to hear about the last act in the saga of the Forester brothers. They would think the story ended when they learned about the two men in the cell.

Cal was one who knew it was not so. The Forester story could never end while Forest Jack was alive. Suddenly he wanted to speak to the Foresters before their limited time ran out. He leapt to the opening in the wall, using the rubble as a jumping off spot. Dropping down into the cell, he glanced from one homely face to the other.

Morgan was already dead. Red had tried to crawl across to him to recover the gun, but his energy had run out. He was alive, but only just. Cal bent over him, and raised the head a little.

'Which of you hombres killed Bob Simpson?'

Red's eyes went to the hole in the wall. He was getting ready to say his last words on earth.

'It was Forest Jack, wasn't it? He wanted funds to spring you!'

Red nodded. 'But you won't ever take him alive. He's too slick, too clever for the lot of you . . .'

Red's voice had grown fainter. It faded altogether. He managed one look of extreme malevolence and then his eyes glazed and his head rolled on his shoulders.

17

Marshal Martin, the town doctor and Simon Perry all arrived together. They poured into the office and found Cal still in the cell, squatting on the bench and reloading his gun. He nodded to Perry's unspoken query as to whether the Foresters were dead, and explained that Larry Raybold had gone in through the front, and that Forest Jack had taken them by surprise by ripping out the back wall.

'Where's Raybold?' Chad Martin asked.

The doctor pushed the others aside before Cal could answer. He was anxious to get Parnes into a better position and to minister to him. Martin and Cal carried him into the office proper and lowered him onto a camp bed.

'That was a good question you asked

back there,' Simon murmured.

Cal said: 'Perhaps we ought to go lookin' for Raybold. He was actin' against the best interests of his old pardners when he went through that hole in the wall. He actually pushed them aside, while he pretended to go after Jack.'

Cal's face looked troubled. Perry had known him long enough to know how his mind worked. 'You think Jack will have dealt with him an' left him about some place, Cal?'

'That's my opinion,' Cal admitted.

Martin provided lamps, and the three of them set off together, moving around the fronts of the nearest buildings and then scouring the alleys which kept them apart and finally working their way across the vacant lots between Main and Second Street.

Chad Martin was the one to discover the body. He stumbled over it as he was negotiating a garbage can in an alley off Second Street. Raybold's corpse was draped around the bottom of the can, and there was something about the expression which made the town marshal gasp as he bent over the body and lowered his lamp to examine it.

Cal and Simon quickly joined him. One of them jostled the body and the hat fell off. Raybold's last expression was a fearful one. He had been stabbed very cleanly through the ribs to the heart, but the unusual thing about him was the new mark on his forehead.

A crude pattern had been scratched there with the point of the killer's knife.

'What is it?' Martin breathed, looking from one lamplit face to the other.

Perry shrugged. 'In a way, you could say it's the signature of the murderer. He meant it to look like a tree, but he was in a hurry an' probably had to scratch it on in the dark. If he'd had more time, he'd have done more detail, two or three trees probably, an' then you might have guessed. His sign is really supposed to indicate a forest.'

'Forest Jack!' Martin ejaculated.

Perry nodded, and Cal said: 'He'll

want revenge for the deaths of his brothers. I'll be the one he'll seek out, so it wouldn't be kind to hide myself away in town. I'll be returnin' to the Circle S in the next half hour.'

Federal Marshal Perry would have done a great deal to prevent Cal from facing up to the last big challenge which was sure to come, but he knew that Cal would answer when the call came because he thought it was his duty. That being so, the friends parted company shortly afterwards, going their respective ways.

It was still dark when Cal reached the ranch house, but he found lights on there and his kid sister sobbing her heart out. As soon as she started to unburden herself, Cal told her something of the happenings in town.

'All our enemies are accounted for now, except one man. The one with the mouth harp. If we keep our wits about us he won't be able to take his revenge, an' then everything will be like it used to be, except that Bob's no longer with us. So how about goin' back to bed now? I'll sleep outside your door, if you like.'

Mollie showed a great deal of affection to Cal, and she asked two or three times after the health of Simon Perry. Eventually she went to bed and slept quite soundly for three hours. Cal also slept.

At a late hour, he roused himself and found the hands waiting for his instructions. Backed by the family he assembled them all and gave them the gist of what had happened in town. Some seemed doubtful about Raybold's duplicity, but they certainly listened when Cal described the appearance of Forest Jack, and explained to them how they were to neglect their normal duties and protect the home buildings and personnel.

Armed men ringed all the buildings at intervals, while Cal himself rode out to north range and brought in the untouched body and belongings of Juan Torres. On the way back, he told his admiring followers some details of the battle at the line shack. None doubted his ability any more, or his manliness.

He was tall in the saddle as far as they were concerned, and anything he said to them was law.

Early in the afternoon when his parents were both taking a nap, he went along with Mollie to the scene of Bob's grave, a giant cottonwood about one hundred yards away from the house. There he brooded for a half hour. Without telling Mollie anything of what was in his mind, he sought to draw courage for the clash which he felt sure would come that night. Mollie watched him mutely and offered up a silent prayer for his constant safety.

As the sun started to dip in the evening, Cal underlined his orders of the morning.

'Don't let anyone by you all through the night, unless it's me. The man we're expectin', Forest Jack, was right here in among the buildings and no one heard him come or go except my sister,

Mollie, and Larry Raybold. So keep a close watch, an' if your eyes start to close, holler for a relief, because this watchin' sure has to be done well.'

Every man swore that he would carry out the instructions to the letter. Henry Simpson stamped about with a more pronounced stoop and a brow quite furrowed with wrinkles. He had grown to hate the name of Forester and Forest Jack, in the short time he had known of the outlaws' existence.

At a comparatively early hour, the guards went to their stations and the family to their bedrooms.

Cal stretched out on his bed with his hat and boots off, brooding over many things. He wondered, for instance, where Simon Perry was and how he had occupied himself during the day. No message had come from town, and the Circle S had seemed like a small private fort with its own retainers. Simon was not the type to be other than busy. He had a slight wound but that would not keep him inactive. Cal tried to put himself into the position of his friend, in an effort to know what he might be doing.

He thought he might be prowling about somewhere, but he could hardly be anywhere near the Circle S without the people at the home buildings knowing. Besides, the party which had been to the shack on north range had covered quite a bit of territory, and they had seen no one.

An hour after dusk, Cal slopped water over his face and neck. He pulled on his boots, stuck his hat on his head and checked the mechanism of his Winchester and .45 Colt. He had plenty of ammunition and both weapons had been specially oiled by his father earlier in the day.

After collecting his gear, he moved out to the stable where the sorrel was waiting for him. Seated in a corner was an effigy of himself, a figure stuffed with paper and cloth and wearing another set of his clothes. For good measure, the hat which had belonged to

Bob, and which had brought about Torres' death, was stuck on the stuffed man's head.

It even had a gun belt on, though the Colt revolver in the holster was not loaded. This effigy was Cal's effort to pull the wool over the eyes of a man with superb night vision. He was hoping that Jack would not be quite so spry this night, on account of his activities the night before.

The harp music came about ten minutes later. The unmistakable sounds of 'Dixie' floated across the range from somewhere to the north-west. Not the distant northwest of the far boundary, but closer. Perhaps half a mile or just a little further away from the clustered buildings. Cal felt himself tense up as he heard it. For a few seconds, his neck hairs prickled, and then he recovered himself.

He put the effigy on the sorrel's back and tried to accustom the gelding to the unusual rider. After adjusting the saddle, he mounted up himself behind the stuffed man and the animal gradually came to accept the new order.

The thing about an effigy on horseback is to keep its back straight and not have it lolling about. Cal knew this, and he made a special effort to control it. As he rode out of the stable, a young hand named Sam Barton made an excuse to have him dismount again. He did so, looking puzzled. Out of the corner of his eye, he saw Roxy Barton, the first man's brother, take a swing at him. Moving easily, Cal blocked it and dropped Roxy to the ground with a crsip punch.

The anger died out in him when he realized that these two youngsters, both under twenty-one, had wanted to take his place so as to protect him from the danger ahead. He apologized and promised to teach both brothers to box when he had a little time in hand.

The incident faded as he rode forth. He knew that he was being led in the direction of a small shallow creek they had used as small children. Alongside of the creek was a wooden hut, where he and Bob had often camped out alone in summer.

A recurrence of the tune 'Dixie' drew him steadily nearer the creek and the ambush which Forest Jack was setting up for him. As the doubly burdened horse topped the slight rise which dominated the approach to the creek meadow, the first accurate bullet flew from the deadly Sharps. From well over a hundred yards away it ripped straight through the stuffed effigy, emerging at the back and narrowly missing Cal, who was making a real effort to keep the other in place.

Grabbing all he needed in the way of weapons, he contrived to fall backwards to the ground, taking his things with him. As soon as he hit the ground, he sprawled, as though dead, and only moved after two minutes to throw a small stone in order to encourage the startled sorrel to go further down the meadow. Fortunately, it obliged.

After this, Cal was going to crawl in.

He had seen from the muzzle flash of the Sharps that Jack was further around the crest of the meadow hollow, and well away from the shack. Perhaps that would be all the intimation he would have of Jack's presence until the Sharps sent along another message of death.

Cal started his crawling approach, and kept it up with only brief spells of inactivity to get back his breath. Some ten minutes later, another blast from the deadly gun sent the stuffed man sailing out of the saddle and dumped him on the ground. The horse flinched, changed direction and started back the way it had arrived.

Jack's second shot had been from beyond the shack, and much deeper in the hollow. Where he would go from there was anybody's guess, but he would certainly use the shack, if he could.

The sorrel pulled up fifty yards from its master and cautiously tore up a few mouthfuls of grass. As its neck straightened out, it scented its master's presence and began to pick its way towards him. Cal flicked a stone to distract it, but the damage was done.

Almost at once the Sharps did a vicious kick against its master's shoulder. Another bullet whined through the air, homing on a rock within inches of Cal's head. Chips and splinters flew in his face, making him hurriedly close his eyes and drop his head.

A second shell buried itself in the ground, under his raised left shoulder. He braced himself for the third and possibly the last of the shots needed to finish him off. To his surprise the blast was scattered. Other guns were booming. He counted four, or perhaps five.

Several rounds were fired by all of them, but the Sharps was silent. A thud was followed by an exclamation of surprise.

'We've got him, Marshal!'

'Be extremely cautious as you approach him, my friend. Better let me come first.'

The second voice was that of Simon

Perry. It was good to hear him back on the job and in charge again. Suddenly Cal's fears left him. He rose to his feet and stumbled forward towards the house, hearing further cries and bits of explanation.

Forest Jack, in an effort to finally eliminate Cal, had clambered up a rope and taken his position on the roof of the building. The thud had been his body falling. He had been hit by no less than four shells. Perry reached him when he had only just died. The longbladed knife was in his hand as though he had planned to use it on the first man near him.

There was no doubt at all about his being dead. Jack had made his last lone play, and lost. Simon and Cal greeted each other warmly, and with great relief. Cal had a fine line of blood down his cheek, from a splinter of stone which had grazed the flesh; otherwise he was unhurt. There were no casualties among the six men who had volunteered, unpaid, to go along with the federal marshal on the off-chance that Jack might turn up in the meadow nearest to the home buildings.

Perry's gamble had been at odds, but it had paid off.

As they rounded up the horses, Perry remembered something he had seen earlier.

'Who was that other poor fellow shot out of the saddle back there?'

'Don't worry,' Cal said with a dry chuckle, 'he's a dummy dressed in my clothes. He took a Sharps bullet right through him and never so much as flinched. Come to think of it, he was the third man wearin' that hat to be hit by the Sharps. And now he's the last.'

'An' that sure is a relief,' Simon remarked, with great feeling.

The two friends mounted up without waiting for the other men. At the top of the hollow they paused long enough to glance back. The rest were on their way with Forest Jack draped over his own buckskin.

'Planted at the far end of Boot Hill,

alongside of his half brothers, he'll make quite an item for visitors to see in town,' Cal commented thoughtfully.

Perry was more philosophical. He said: 'I wonder if the stories about him will grow, now that he's dead, or whether he'll be gradually forgotten.'

'Who knows? One thing I do know, though, Simon. He's a good man to see buried!'

THE END

We do hope that you have enjoyed reading this large print book.

Did you know that all of our titles are available for purchase?

We publish a wide range of high quality large print books including:
Romances, Mysteries, Classics
General Fiction
Non Fiction and Westerns

Special interest titles available in large print are:
The Little Oxford Dictionary
Music Book, Song Book
Hymn Book, Service Book

Also available from us courtesy of Oxford University Press:
Young Readers' Dictionary
(large print edition)
Young Readers' Thesaurus
(large print edition)

For further information or a free brochure, please contact us at:
Ulverscroft Large Print Books Ltd.,
The Green, Bradgate Road, Anstey,
Leicester, LE7 7FU, England.
Tel: (00 44) **0116 236 4325**
Fax: (00 44) **0116 234 0205**

Other titles in the
Linford Western Library:

WEST OF EDEN

Mike Stall

Marshal Jack Adams was tired of people shooting at him. So when the kid came into town sporting a two-gun rig and out to make his reputation — at Adams' expense — it was time to turn in his star and buy that horse ranch he'd dreamed about in the Eden Valley. It looked peaceful, but the valley was on the verge of a range-war and there was only one man to stop it. So Adams pinned on a star again and started shooting back — with a vengeance!

BAR 10 GUNSMOKE

Boyd Cassidy

As always, Bar 10 rancher Gene Adams responded to a plea for help, taking Johnny Puma and Tomahawk. They headed into Mexico to help their friend Don Miguel Garcia. But they were walking into a trap laid by the outlaw known as Lucifer. When the Bar 10 riders arrived at Garcia's ranch, Johnny was cut down in a hail of bullets. Adams and Tomahawk thunder into action to take on Lucifer and his gang. But will they survive the outlaws' hot lead?

THE FRONTIERSMEN

Elliot Conway

Major Philip Gaunt and his former batman, Naik Alif Khan, veterans of dozens of skirmishes on British India's north-west frontier, are fighting the wild and dangerous land of northern Mexico. Aided by 'Buckskin' Carlson, a newly reformed drunk, they are hunting down Mexican bandidos who murdered the major's sister. But it proves to be a dangerous trail. Death by knife and gun is never far away. Will they finally deliver cold justice to the bandidos?

A BULLET FOR MISS ROSE

Scott Dingley

In the aftermath of a bank robbery in Terlingua, Rose Morrison lies dead. Assigned to pursue her killer, Ranger Parker Burden learns that the chief suspect is the son of his friend, Don Vicente Hernandez. Teamed with a Pinkerton detective, Parker pursues Angel Hernandez to Mexico, shadowed by bounty hunters. They become mixed up with the tyrannical General Ortega and uncover a sinister conspiracy. There is a bloody showdown, but has Parker found the one who fired the fatal bullet at Miss Rose?